To DAYTON:

The

Royal

Tournament

Richard H. Stephens.

The Royal Tournament

The Royal Tournament

The Royal Tournament by Richard H. Stephens

http://www.richardhstephens.com/

Cover Art by Marco Pennacchietti

Paperback ISBN: 978-1-775-1036-1-5

The Royal Tournament

The Royal Tournament

Publication has been a long time in coming. I would like to say thank you to all my Beta readers: Caroline Davidson, Jordan Brown, Joshua Stephens, Louise Spilsbury, Paul Stephens and Ralph Phelan for your invaluable help in making my fantasy become a reality.

Throughout the end stages of the writing process I found, quite by chance, an artist of unsurpassable talent. Thank you Marco Pennacchietti for your patience and your vision in bringing my characters to life. You can check out his amazing artwork at: https://www.artstation.com/deimos23390 or contact him directly at: pennacchietti23marco@gmail.com

I would also like to say thank you to David M. Kelly who came to my rescue as I floundered within the daunting world of publishing. Thanks for your patient guidance. David is a Canadian Author who writes Science Fiction. For more on David M. Kelly, check out his website at: http://davidmkelly.net/

Finally, a special note to Horsechickie. Your constant support means more than you'll ever know.

"My treasures do not clink together or glitter, they gleam in the sun and neigh in the night." -*Arabian proverb*

"My Beautiful Angel, you fill me with wonder, ever more each day. You are most truly, heaven sent." -*Alcyonne*

The Royal Tournament

The Royal Tournament

Table of Contents

The Royal Tournament

The Royal Tournament

Chapter 1 - Strange Harvest

"**Javen!** Come quick, boy!"

The boy in question stood up with a start, looking across a great expanse of golden wheat. The voice beckoning him was Jebadiah's, his father. By the distress in his tone, he wasn't calling him to help with a broken wagon wheel or fetch extra twine.

He had seen his father an hour earlier in the northern quarter of their farm where a great river meandered about its perimeter. Javen dropped the pitchfork he had been using and lumbered toward the river in the direction of his father's voice. Behind him stretched a neatly cut row of wheat, heaped and bound every so often in large piles, ready for the wagon.

He neared the farm's edge abutting the riverbank, dreading the thought of finding his father afloat in the river. Approaching his seventeenth birthday, he begrudged the fact he had never learned to swim.

Before the riverbank came into sight he exhaled with relief—his father's head and shoulders visible above the gently swaying golden crop.

His father waved frantically at him.

Javen waved back.

"Get down, boy," His father warned in a hushed voice.

Javen ducked, looking over his shoulder. Bending below the height of the crop, he weaved his way through the stalks until he came across his father lying beside the riverbank, peering through the last row of wheat separating them from the water's edge, tightly clutching his sickle.

"What is it, papa?"

The Royal Tournament

His father pointed across the river at the rolling hillside, to a line of grassy mounds topped by pine trees.

For a few moments, only the tranquil countryside met Javen's stare. He detected movement behind a clump of trees atop one of the higher ridges, a brilliant azure banner rising above its peak; the crest indecipherable from such a distance. As quickly as the billowing pennant appeared, so did its bearer, astride a magnificent white horse. The majestic beast, glimmering in silver plate, and draped in azure and vermillion, matched the pennant and the rider's surcoat. Another horse followed, rider and mount matching the first, then two more, then three. A couple of breaths later, a score of mounted knights rode along the ridge, gleaming in the midday sun, heading south toward Millsford.

"Who are they, papa?" Javen asked, unable to take his eyes off the enchanting procession.

His father remained silent for some time. When the last rider disappeared behind the next ridge, his words caused Javen to jump.

"Don't rightly know, son. They're not from these parts, of that I am certain." He fell silent again before adding, "As far as I can recollect, I have never seen the likes of their markings. I haven't traveled everywhere in this realm, but I reckon they aren't the king's men."

"Do you think there will be trouble in town?"

Jebadiah turned his gaze northward, making certain a rear scout wasn't trailing the host, before he gained his feet.

"Well, the good baron has mentioned more than once that the king is concerned about troops massing along the southern border of the Kraidic Empire, but I doubt he would allow a host this far into the kingdom without offering some sort of opposition. Those men appear too well polished and fresh to have done battle with the king's forces recently."

"Perhaps they slipped through unnoticed?"

"Aye, they may have." His father scratched at his three-day-old beard. "They may have, but I doubt it. Zephyr's border guards patrol the outlying regions with an iron gauntlet. So much so, in fact, that our allies are hesitant to trade with us these days."

Javen stood and attached his sickle to a thong hanging from his belt.

Looking across the river to the spot where the procession had disappeared, his father added, "Best we find out what the good baron knows."

After washing up, and changing into something befitting a baron's audience, Javen and his father hitched a two-horse team to an old buckboard and set off along a hard-packed, dirt path leading south into the town of Millsford. The wagon bounced its riders along the winding trail, careening from rock to rut, between banks of unharvested wheat breasting the lane. Grasshoppers by the hundreds jumped to and fro at their approach, while gnats buzzed about their heads.

A cool east breeze wafted up the road, easing the heat of the day. By the time the great outer wall of the baron's homestead thwarted their progress, the huge orange sun had planted itself firmly upon the peaks of the distant mountain range stretching clear across the western horizon.

Two sentries standing outside a lone portcullis greeted them warmly. Jebadiah told them he wished to speak to the good baron about an urgent matter. The ranking sentry rubbed his lips in thought for a moment before nodding and jumping onto the bench seat beside Javen, directing them forward.

Javen led the team along cobblestone streets lined with merchants stowing their wares for the night. Millsford seemed busier than usual.

The main street terminated at the threshold of another set of gates, bridging a stone wall surrounding the baron's estate proper. The inner wall hummed with the activity of sentries upon its high battlements; the iron gates were shut tight.

Javen brought the team to a halt. The guardsman jumped down to converse with the inner gate sentries. Before long, the gates swung inward, exposing a vast green courtyard of trees and fountains lining pathways twisting about the grounds, adorned in a kaleidoscope of flowers.

"Come with me," the guard escorting them directed, breaking away from all his colleagues but one. "Jonas, here, will mind your wagon."

They walked down a lengthy promenade toward the majestic keep at its other end. Javen's father engaged the sentry in idle talk while they strolled through the lush grounds, passing beneath an immense, iron latticed portcullis and entering a small antechamber inside the keep.

The guard went through a wooden door on the far side of the room, closing it behind him.

Shortly the door opened again, their escort beckoning them to follow. They walked down a vaulted passageway pocked with closed doors, softly lit by flickering sconces. The tapestry lining the hallway served to obscure narrow slits in the wall; murder holes protecting the egress. The hallway ended at an open set of massive oak doors.

Backless benches ran the length of the hall beyond, their ranks broken by a slender aisle traversing its midst. At the hall's far end, a large table set with half a dozen high-backed chairs faced the empty pews.

"Seat yourself in the front row, Jebadiah. The good baron shall be with you momentarily." The guard motioned to the empty bench before closing the door on his way out.

They didn't have to wait long. The baron of Millsford entered through a small doorway behind the table. They stood out of respect, watching the short, gray-haired man manoeuvre his considerable girth around the chairs. They dropped to one knee.

The baron's deep, monotone voice echoed loudly in the vacant chamber, "There is no need of formality here, Jeb. We are friends, alone, amongst ourselves."

Javen and his father rose to receive the baron's meaty handshake, the man's balding pate catching the flickering glare of the many rush lights lining the walls.

The Royal Tournament

With Jebadiah's bidding, Javen fetched the baron a chair from the far side of the table, placing it before the pews so the baron could relieve his bowed legs.

After exchanging pleasantries, the baron asked, "So, Jeb, what brings you to town during harvest? You are too busy to be paying me a social visit; though don't get me wrong, your company is surely welcome."

"Thank you, sir," Jebadiah said. He paused, uncertain of what kind of tact to employ. When he spoke, his knitted brow informed the baron this visit was anything but social. "Is there any trouble about?"

The baron frowned. "No. What would make you ask that?"

"'Tis probably nothing."

"But?"

"While working the north field this morning, we watched a host of fully armoured knights moving through the hills across the river, coming this way. Their pennants bore no semblance to any I know."

The baron leaned back into his seat, studying the two. He pulled thoughtfully upon his lower lip. The faint perception of a smile pulled at the corners of his mouth. Without warning, he let forth a hearty roar.

Jebadiah looked on in confusion. He didn't think the news he had taken the time to deliver, amusing.

The large man slapped his thighs. "Oh Jebadiah, you are a godsend. Your fidelity is irreproachable. Even during peacetime, you ward my flank."

"I don't think I understand."

"No, of course you don't, my good friend, of course you don't," the baron chuckled. "Forgive me. I should have realized that while the rest of my great homestead prepares to receive our blessed king, my hardest working vassal has not had time to hear of the joyous event."

The baron had Javen's undivided attention. "The king? Coming to Millsford?"

The baron overlooked Javen's slight of forgetting to address him properly.

Jebadiah didn't. He shot his son a dark look. He had taught Javen better than that.

The Royal Tournament

The baron laughed, his hands cupping his large belly, "Do not admonish young Javen, Jeb. He is excited, naturally." He considered Javen's eager eyes. "Aye, young Milford, his grace shall arrive by Michaelmas. Escorted by Zephyr's finest knights to participate in the royal tournament. Hosted this year, in Millsford."

Javen's eyes threatened to pop from his face. He gaped, but not a sound escaped him.

Jebadiah retained his formal composure. "It is unexpected news indeed, good baron. I thought his grace had chosen Ember Breath for this year's tournament?"

The baron became serious. "Nay, Jeb. Your information is correct, or I should say, was. A grievous storm swept in from the Zephyr Sea over a fortnight ago, inflicting great damage along the coast. So much so, in fact, it has rendered Ember Breath unsuitable to stage the royal festivities. I have dispatched as many people as I deemed expendable to aid our southern friends. That said, their misfortune has proven very propitious to Millsford."

Jebadiah furrowed his brow. "This is the first I have heard, good baron. Is there anything we can do to assist? Perhaps I can send a wagon train of wheat to help feed the people. Our crop is nearly in. With your leave, I volunteer Javen and myself to go hither and lend whatever aid possible."

What? Javen was appalled. The king was in Millsford. That in itself was an event that hadn't happened during his short lifetime, and his father had the audacity to volunteer him to miss the occasion.

Javen wasn't a selfish person by nature. He felt bad for the people in the south, but he had his future to consider. He didn't care to follow in his father's footsteps pushing a plow for the rest of his life. He dreamed of making his way to the house of Zephyr to join the royal guard.

For years he had participated in local tournaments, showing himself well. Ever since seeing his first jousting match, he fantasized about participating in the Royal Tournament, but the great festival always took place during harvest time, and his father couldn't afford to lose Javen's hands. It was just the two of them since mama died.

The Royal Tournament

With the tournament taking place in Millsford this year and the harvest almost in, he could participate in his favourite event, the joust, and still keep up with his chores. He stared vehemently at his father.

The baron returned to his jovial self, his great smile but another fold in the fat of his cheeks. "Your offer is duly noted Jeb, and I thank you on behalf of our Ember Breath contingent, but I need your services here."

The baron paused, noticing Javen's relief. "I am counting on your crops to supply this tournament, as most of our other staples have already been delegated to the relief envoy. Besides," the baron clasped his hands together and looked directly into Javen's brown eyes. "I am personally counting on young Javen here to represent Millsford."

Javen's eyes bulged. "Me? Really?"

Jebadiah shot his son a disdainful look; Javen again forgetting the expected formality required of addressing the baron. His attempt to say so was cut off by the baron, whose attention lay squarely on Javen.

"Aye, you." The baron slapped Javen's knee. "You have won the area tournaments for the last three years running in the junior category. It's time you entered the men's category."

"I would be honoured, but—"

"But nothing. It is my opinion you are not only ready; you are worthy. In fact, Captain Korn, the head of our meager delegation, has personally selected you. You should be honoured."

"Oh, I am, good baron. I shan't disappoint you," Javen's voice squeaked, it was so tight.

The colour returned to Jebadiah's face. A slight smile replaced his frown. He always felt responsible for Javen having to miss the Royal Tournament, but there were more important things in life than silly boys' games of derring-do. The baron's jolly voice brought his attention back to the meeting hall.

"I don't expect you will, young Milford. In fact, I expect you will do very well. Especially if you conduct yourself anything like your father did in his youth."

The Royal Tournament

Javen gulped.

The baron laughed and said to Jebadiah, "Now get the boy home and train him up the best you can. The tournament commences six days from now. The lists will dominate the first day so get that fine horse of yours ready as well."

The Royal Tournament

Chapter 2-Training Day

Javen couldn't get the vision of the gleaming cavalcade that had recently rode past the farm out of his mind. It was the day his life began to change.

It was a hot day, the second day since their meeting with the baron. He and his father were taking a break from harvesting the wheat; the field they'd been cutting, now all spiky stubble and sheaves that lay waiting to be bundled for transport to the threshing barn. A line of willows marked the southern edge of the field. The trees leaned out over the river where green-blue dragonflies skipped across the water. The air was dense with the smell of plants and sweat. Cicadas buzzed in the distance.

'Taking a break' meant that his father sat on a boulder, resting his aches and calling out instructions while Javen worked, training in earnest for the upcoming tournament. Today, they were drilling with his jousting horse, Sunseeker.

"More speed!"

His father shaded his eyes, squinting as Javen put his heels to Sunseeker's glossy sides, urging him into a hard gallop. Beside them, Rusty, their dog, tried to keep pace, tongue flapping about, barking encouragement.

"All right, now imagine your opponent is cheating and aiming for a head shot. What do you do?"

Javen twisted his body, angling his weight perilously over the left stirrup while making sure Sunseeker continued in a straight line. He ducked his head to the side and then snaked his weight back into the saddle before reining Sunseeker to a stop.

"Yes!" Javen pumped his fist triumphantly in the air. "I got it this time, didn't I?"

The Royal Tournament

"That was good," his father said. "But it will be harder when you're burdened down with armour. Tomorrow we will outfit you in your mail and breastplate."

Javen grinned. His father hadn't let him wear the armour since the local tournament in the spring, insisting that the priority was to work on Sunseeker's training. The horse had rushed the tilts back then, barely in control. Today Sunseeker was eager, his breaths pushing out against Javen's legs, but he softened obediently to Javen's hand.

Jebadiah rose stiffly and hobbled over to pat Sunseeker's neck. The horse's black coat was damp with exertion. Jebadiah was damp too. He didn't handle the heat as well as he used to.

Javen worried, noticing the pinched look around his father's mouth. His father's old leg wound from the war he'd fought at Baron Millsford's side, obviously bothered him more than usual.

"I'll fetch us some lunch, and then we can get back to work," Jebadiah said, ambling toward the house in the distance.

Back at the barn, Javen dismounted and removed his old saddle from Sunseeker's back. After rubbing him down with a knot of straw, Javen led him into the cool confines of his stall. Securing the door behind him, Javen grabbed a softly burning lantern from a peg in the wall and made his way to the storage room at the rear of the barn.

The hinges on the room's door squealed as he opened it. The lantern's glow illuminated the dusty equipment inside the large room. His skin tingled with excitement. A large chest, buried behind rusty farm implements and dusty lances of various sizes, drew his attention. Aligning the lances in the aisle outside and setting aside the old scythes and broken pieces of harrows, he knelt in front of the chest and blew the dust from its lid.

Inside the musty trunk lay his various collection of armour. His father's really, but it now belonged to him. Hopefully this year it would fit better. He had grown taller and filled in a lot more since the last time he had donned the dented and rusted equipment.

That had been in the spring during the local tournament held at the end of planting season, to celebrate the new crops. He had won the jousting event, and was runner-up in the crossbow competition, but overall, he hadn't faired as well as he had hoped. If he wished to make the king's men notice him he would have to do better. Unfortunately, melee fighting wasn't in his makeup. He had nearly lost his head the last time.

The baron expected great things of him, expecting him to pick up where his father left off twenty years before.

Jebadiah had been a prize tournament fighter. Many said that had the Kraidic wars not intervened, he might have become 'Emperor of the Field,' the prestigious title awarded to the overall victor of the annual Royal Tournament.

Becoming Emperor of the Field meant more than the prize money awarded at local tournaments. Emperor of the Field meant the king and his personal guard would be calling upon their service, more than likely enlisting them and training them at Castle Svelte, the royal seat of the kingdom.

Nerves clutched Javen's stomach. Tomorrow he would ask his father to help him practice with the hammer. Swords were for skinnier, faster moving men. Cudgels suited bigger men. Besides, his father had made a name for himself swinging his prized hammer for King Peter's father.

At the bottom of the chest, wrapped caringly in oily rags, lay the weapon in question. With more than a little trepidation, Javen pulled the heavy bundle free. Unwrapping the large headed hammer, he stared at the familiar etchings along the side of the metal head.

He sighed. Who was he kidding. He was a marksman, not an infantryman. In a tournament of this size, the list of notable entrants vying for the eye of the king would be lengthy. He would be lucky to make it through the first round.

He had three more days to prepare. What he lacked in aptitude he would have to make up for in strength. Of that he had plenty, but he would be facing grown men who made their living swinging a weapon for their overlords. There would certainly be men much stronger than himself.

Stepping out the back door into the paddock he swung the hammer about, trying to get used to the heft again. In the spring tournament, he had misjudged what would happen were he to miss his opponent and found himself almost falling over as he tried to maintain his grip on the cumbersome weapon. His opponent, armed with a saber and small shield, had made quick work of his clumsiness.

Rusty's enthusiastic barking sounded at the front of the barn and continued through the open passageway between the numerous stalls. His father's voice sounded above the dog, "Javen! Dinner's ready!"

"Coming papa!" Javen dropped the grisly hammerhead to the dirt. Three days. That wasn't enough time to even work in the muscles required to wield the weapon properly, let alone get comfortable with it again.

Rusty burst onto the paddock and circled him, barking like a fool.

"Ya, ya, boy. I'm coming."

Javen followed the dog back into the barn and stood the hammer against the inside wall of the storage room. Before grabbing the lantern and walking away he studied his father's armour. There would be new dents on it before the week was out. Of that he had no doubt.

The Royal Tournament

Chapter 3 - Inaugural Joust

Tournament day dawned cool and clear.

Jebadiah pulled up on the reins of the two plow horses leading their buckboard toward town. Steam billowed from their nostrils as they crested the last hill before Millsford and stamped to a stop. The town was cast in early morning shadow, but it wasn't dormant. Jebadiah got to his feet and stared, unprepared for the spectacle below.

Millsford was built into the heart of a large basin where the surging waters of the Canorous River met the subtle flow of the mighty Madrigail, converging in a flurry of spray and foam. With its northern and western borders flanked by water, the town stretched southeast to the base of a ridge rising from the river basin, half a league west of the ford. A low outer wall encircled the town between the two separate riverbanks at the base of the ridge.

Within the low walls, a sprawling tent city had been erected. Tarpaulin structures of all shapes, sizes and colours were crammed together so tightly he couldn't imagine walking between them, let alone trying to navigate his buckboard amongst the throng. The higher peaks of the permanent buildings endeavoured to climb out from underneath the crush of man and beast.

From Jebadiah's vantage point, both rivers stretched eastward into the rolling countryside. Along each bank, a separate road entered the town through the only two breaches in the wooden palisade.

The roads teemed with approaching traffic, appearing from this distance to be great, writhing serpents coiled upon the rivers' banks attempting to squeeze through the barbicans to wreak havoc with the smaller snakes of milling people within.

Prodded by the drivers of wagons coming up from behind them, laden with supplies and colourful people from every corner of

The Royal Tournament

Zephyr and beyond, Jebadiah waved a good morning to all, and urged his team forward.

As they descended into the jowls of mayhem, Javen sat in the back of the wagon, facing the rear amid a jumble of tack and weaponry, equipment and fancy clothing. Oblivious to the turmoil going on around him, he busily mended and polished his tournament gear.

Nearing the southern gatehouse, the procession slowed to a crawl, but Javen didn't notice until his black horse, tethered to the rear of the buckboard, whinnied.

Looking up from his preparation, Javen was awestruck. A plethora of various sized wagons surrounded him farther than he could see. The resulting din threatened to crush him as his senses attuned to their surroundings. He craned his neck to observe the outer wall, fifty paces ahead. Pennants from all over the world flapped lazily in the soft, morning breeze.

His father's smiling visage commanded his attention.

"Well, my boy, you've finally made it."

Javen could only nod, his throat tight. His father laughed and urged the team forward with a lurch. They passed beneath the portcullis into bedlam.

Captain Korn appeared out of nowhere, motioning for Jebadiah to follow. The captain paused long enough to welcome Javen to the Royal Tournament, smiling when Javen mustered a squeaky thank you.

Captain Korn's presence commanded respect in Millsford. Years ago, he fought many battles as a lesser knight in the king's army, acclaiming himself well. As a reward for his valiant services, he was bestowed a plot of land near Millsford where his family bred warhorses for the royal guard. Although of average height, his broad shoulders and thick chest bespoke volumes. A groomed, pointed, brown goatee highlighted his chiseled facial features. He surveyed the multitude of men and beasts parting before them, allowing them to proceed unimpeded toward the inner wall. The guard, tripled on the interior gatehouses, didn't dare to slow their progress.

The Royal Tournament

Arriving the previous day, the king's men stood about in knots within the baron's courtyard, watching knights sparring with nobles, all in mail and polished armour.

It was Captain Korn's turn to show his respect, as he led his charges amongst the king's men.

The baron, anticipating their arrival, stood upon a broad, stone porch. He smiled, greeted Jebadiah warmly and said, "Ah, my champion has arrived. In the days to come, young Javen will bring the king's mighty war machine to its knees, you will see."

Javen jumped from the wagon, and promptly fell upon his face. Wide-eyed, he offered the baron a tight smile as he caught himself with his hands on the ground.

The baron cupped his belly. "I see your nerves have robbed your voice. Come inside and relax if you can. Your first battle is scheduled for just before the midday feast."

The baron turned to enter his stronghold. Two knights snapped to attention and opened the heavy doors. Without looking back, he added, "Korn, see to their wagon."

Korn gaped at the baron's receding girth. With a grunt, he took the reins from Jebadiah. When the doors closed, he delegated the task to one of the men standing guard.

The noonday sun parched the throats of amassed dignitaries and assembled guests seated along the perimeter of the jousting field in the great courtyard behind the baron's manor. Large banners depicting the king's coat of arms: a golden eagle with wings poised for landing, clenching a sword in its talons, beautifully embroidered upon a vermillion background, flapped lazily above the crowd. Alongside the king's banner were those of Millsford, Madrigail Bay, Gritian and pretty well every other town in Zephyr. Interspersed with the local pennants, the flags of neighbouring kingdoms swearing allegiance to King Peter snapped in unison.

The Royal Tournament

The crowd buzzed with excitement, anticipating the next joust. All eyes were upon the northern ready tent. As one, the spectators rose to their feet in a thunderous ovation. Prince Malcolm's retainers pulled open the tent flaps and led his ebony stallion onto the grounds. Firerider's glistening flanks rippled beneath its proud rider.

Prince Malcolm, not yet eighteen, had won the Royal Tournament two years running, defeating the king's champion at Madrigail Bay to assume the honourific title, Emperor of the Field. He raised his polished lance in salute to the crowd. They roared even louder.

His squire, a teenage boy with long black hair and bewitching ice-blue eyes, handed him Firerider's reins and then checked the saddle cinches. Satisfied his knight's gear was properly fitted, the squire bowed deeply and scurried back into the tent.

The prince scrutinized the crowd, his lance held easy. Smiling, he hailed the contestant waiting within the southern ready tent, following the protocol for pageantry.

"Enter God's blessed field, meek challenger, if thou darest," the prince called out. "Ride forth and know thee well, today ye shall be bested by the Emperor of the Field."

The cheering crowd craned its collective neck. The two huge tent flaps of the southern pavilion opened outward. Two squires rushed to get out of the way as the challenger's roan trotted onto the tilting field.

The newcomer's sun bright, yellow surcoat rippled above the rider's polished armour, depicting the Cliff Face coat of arms. Riding out to meet the Emperor, the Cliff Face knight reined in alongside Firerider. Custom dictated that anyone challenging the Emperor of the Field must offer to surrender their lance without challenge.

Bowing low over his pommel the challenger tendered his lance, handle first. "I submit to thee without contest my lance and my honour, should my Emperor decree."

The Emperor of the Field placed his left hand upon the lance handle. "Brave challenger, I would not dishonour your coat of arms without contest. Should ye decide to withdraw from the tournament, I shan't begrudge your courage. What say ye, o noble warrior?"

The Royal Tournament

The challenger pulled his lance back. Grasping the helmet resting upon his saddle horn, he donned the feather plumed, conical headpiece, and flipped open the faceplate. "I say nay, good Emperor. I wish thee luck, for thou shalt have gravest need." With that said, the knight from Cliff Face closed his faceplate in defiance.

The Emperor of the Field fitted his own, round topped, vermillion plumed helm over his head and proclaimed, "Then I say, ware thee well, foolish knave." He proceeded to address the gathering, "Let the joust commence."

The crowd cheered as the two riders turned their mounts to face the royal box, built at ground level into the eastern stand, its awning ablaze with the dominant heraldic coat-of-arms of the king's house. Two knights resplendent in suits of gleaming plate stood guard, bearing large halberds, one on either side of the king's box.

King Peter regarded the contestants for a moment. With a nod, he gave them leave to assume their respective starting places.

Within the northern pavilion, Javen stood spread eagle, peering through a crack in the tent flaps, gazing out onto the jousting field.

Behind him, Captain Korn barked orders at the squires who were busy trying to fit Javen's badly dented armour, while two grooms outfitted Javen's warhorse with its protective plating and colourful mantle.

Korn took in the spectacle of the squires' ordeal as they tried unsuccessfully to steady Javen's limbs long enough to put his gear on.

Javen watched in awe as Prince Malcolm cantered Firerider toward him. He moved away from the tent flaps for fear the prince would catch him staring, the action eliciting a chorus of groans and curses from his attendants.

Captain Korn noticed his young charge's knees tremble, the plate armour clinking rhythmically. He smiled at the exasperated attendants attempts to fit Javen's surcoat over his stiff arms—the back of the golden surcoat bearing the Milford coat of arms: a sword breaking upon a chaff of wheat, alongside the label denoting Javen as Jebadiah's first-born son.

Korn had seen Javen joust in local tournaments many times before. The boy was good. He couldn't recall seeing Javen as nervous as this before, but appearing before the king for the first time was certainly a big deal.

Suddenly, from without, a great roar arose. Javen shrugged off his retainers, who in turn threw their arms up in disgust, beseeching Captain Korn's aid.

The captain laughed.

Javen slit the tent flaps in time for he and his aides to receive a face full of upturned turf as Firerider dug in and charged down the tilting rail.

Javen absently shook off the dirt, his attention riveted upon the ensuing collision.

Prince Malcolm rode upright at full gallop, the tip of his lance poised above his vermillion plumed helm, much to the delight of the ladies in attendance.

The combatant from Cliff Face bore down on him, hunched over his pommel, lance at the ready.

Javen's eyes grew wide.

Twenty paces separated the combatants. Ten paces. Five paces and still the prince rode erect, as if gallivanting across the countryside.

Just before contact, the prince's lance dipped to level, his body lowering over Firerider's neck in one fluid motion, deftly intercepting his quarry's lance with his shield. A resounding clang and the crack of splintering wood marked the collision. The prince drove his lance into his opponent's breastplate, unhorsing him.

The assembled mass cheered, watching the Emperor of the Field rein in Firerider.

The Royal Tournament

The prince lifted his faceplate and proclaimed, "I take thee as my prisoner."

The knight from Cliff Face struggled to catch his breath. He rolled to his stomach with the help of his retainers. Gaining his knees with the difficulty afforded by his armour, he offered homage to his captor, "I succumb to thee, Emperor. Do unto me no further grief."

Clad in green and red patchwork livery, the local town crier announced the next combatants.

The baron of Millsford sat proudly behind the king's box. Beside him, a nervous Jebadiah held his breath as his son's retainers pulled open the northern pavilion tent flaps. Protocol allowed for the knight with the highest prestige, whether he be royal, reigning champion, or from the tournament's hometown, to occupy the northern pavilion. The honour allowed said knight to enter the jousting field first and call out his adversary.

Captain Korn led Javen's steed, Sunseeker, onto the battlefield. Sunseeker, a stunning black warhorse, the pride of Millsford, demanded the king's notice, resplendent in a great, golden surcoat matching its rider.

The crowd voraciously cheered their local entrant. The nerves Javen experienced earlier were nothing compared to those binding him up now. He knew at least half of the crowd personally, but at this moment, their presence provided him little solace. They may as well have been archbishops and kings.

He sat upon his horse in front of the king's box, facing the king himself, the clamour of the crowd a distant thought as King Peter's eyes caught his own. He felt his face redden. He had forgotten to call out his adversary.

The king's expectant gaze didn't do him any favours.

King Peter's gaze softened, feeling for the young man. He smiled and nodded slightly.

The Royal Tournament

That little gesture proved enough to break the spell. Swallowing the lump in his throat, Javen hoisted his lance in salute to Zephyr's monarch.

The expectant crowd fell silent.

Javen accepted Sunseeker's reins from his retainers, who in turn, hightailed it from the field.

Captain Korn offered him a salute and a wink, before following the others.

Javen turned his mount to face the southern pavilion. With more than a little trepidation, evidenced by the squeak in his voice, he called forth his competitor, "Enter God's blessed field, meek challenger, if thou darest. Ride forth and know thee well, ye shall face the wrath of the chaff. The eternal giver of life in a world where mere men such as thee simply come hither to wither with the passing season." He hoped that didn't sound as corny as it felt.

The crowd shouted, "Huzzah," and turned their collective heads to the southern pavilion.

A pair of grooms pulled aside the tent flap, making way for their master.

The knight, clad in gleaming, golden armour, pranced his ivory stallion onto the pitch. Both rider and mount were draped in aquamarine surcoats, emblazoned with a waterfall cascading between two mountains: the crest of Songsbirth, Millsford's neighbour to the southeast. The Songsbirthian brought his mount to a halt abreast Javen and attempted to stare him down.

Javen met the leer, his innocent appearance contrasting sharply with his older opponent's grizzled mien.

With the preliminaries underway, Javen felt his nervousness ease as he focused on the task at hand. This was his best event.

The Songsbirthian knight realized his intimidation tactic wasn't working. "I say, ware thee own self well, my farming friend. Let it not be unbeknownst that without the lifeblood of the Madrigail, its parturition in Songsbirth, your chaff would wither and die. Know thee also well, the flood I shall deliver unto you."

The Songsbirthian donned the conical helm resting upon his saddle horn.

The Royal Tournament

Before slipping into his own helmet, Javen proclaimed, "Ware thee well, good challenger, for ye are to know the heart of the chaff, for neither drought nor flood can deny it."

Javen donned his helm, wincing at his last statement. He flipped up his faceplate with a metallic squeal, and said to the entire gathering, "Let the joust commence."

Both riders customarily turned their mounts to face the king, and bowed, offering their lances.

The king stood and nodded for them to assume their respective starting places.

Both riders bowed once again before leading their horses in opposite directions.

Once ready, the participants watched the royal box.

King Peter held a white glove in his outstretched hand. He released it without further ado, signaling the commencement of the joust.

As the glove left the king's hand, the combatants bent low over their mount's neck. They waited until the glove hit the field before spurring to a gallop.

The crowd erupted.

Sunseeker's nostrils flared with the sudden exertion, its flanks rippling with pounding muscles.

Javen gripped his lance tightly, keeping its tip parallel to the ground, perfectly still. Sunseeker ran the rail tight, needing little control from its rider.

With a sudden, resounding collision, the riders met.

The Songsbirthian's lance impacted with Javen's dented shield, the force splintering the shaft.

Javen drove his own lance home, the Songsbirthian catching it with the edge of his shield. The metal coronal protecting the pole's tip deflected up, catching the knight beneath the chin, its flanged edge lodging itself between the man's gorget and helm.

The Songsbirthian cried out as he flew from his mount, taking Javen's lance with him, his hands clutching at his neck.

Javen struggled to remain in his saddle, his lance pulled from his grasp. He heard the excitement of the crowd at his victory, but he wasn't happy. He'd been lucky. The Songsbirthian had deflected his thrust. Fortunately, the lance tip had snagged itself within his challenger's armour.

Reining in Sunseeker, he trotted back to the king's box to receive his official proclamation of victory.

On his way, he noted the Songsbirthian writhing in pain, surrounded by grooms, and a healer who tended a nasty gash in the knight's neck. Javen steeled himself. It was undoubtedly the most dangerous event in the tournament.

Reaching the royal box, helmet in hand, Javen bowed low over Sunseeker's neck.

The crowd fell silent.

King Peter's booming voice took in the entire gathering, "Well done, young Milford, a noble joust indeed. I declare you victor and offer you a royal ribbon of conquest."

Javen humbly nodded, turning in his saddle to accept his fallen lance from a beaming Captain Korn.

Once rid of the lance, the captain bowed to the king.

Javen offered his lance tip to King Peter, who took it in hand and knotted a short, vermillion ribbon near the coronal.

Javen bowed again. With the king's leave, he turned Sunseeker toward the northern pavilion.

Emerging from underneath the great canopy sheltering the royal box, Javen hefted his lance high to the home crowd's unbridled delight.

Back at the baron's manor, Javen was invited to join both baron and king for the noonday feast, along with forty other notables from Zephyr and beyond.

He sat clear across the banquet hall from the king, Prince Malcolm, Prince Graham, King's Champion Jarr-nash Sylvan Jordic, and the baron; elated to be afforded such an auspicious opportunity.

On Javen's right sat a knight from Serpens, a neighbouring kingdom to the north. The man's azure surcoat was trimmed in

The Royal Tournament

vermillion. Studying the large man, he realized the riders Javen and his father had witnessed crossing the foothills were the Serpensian delegation.

The Serpensian was a huge man. Seated, he was taller than Javen was standing. The giant's long, brown hair and thick beard did nothing to distract from his prominent forehead. His pudgy cheeks displayed deep dimples when he laughed, and being a jovial type, this happened often. His small nose seemed out of place upon his face, flat and obviously broken more than once. He introduced himself as Helvius Pyxis.

A wiry, dark skinned man with tightly curled, black hair sat on Javen's left. He wore only a tanned leather chest protector and a similarly coloured loincloth. A well-used scorpion flail covered with metal barbs hung precariously from the thong cinching his loincloth about his waist. Although the man couldn't speak the language of Zephyr to save his life, he managed to convey the fact he hailed from a distant kingdom south of Zephyr, and his name was Alcyonne.

As near as Javen could tell, the kingdom was called Aldebaran, or something to that effect. Javen had never heard of the place, but he wasn't exactly a man of the world. He took note of the name, however, and made a mental note to find out where this Aldebaran was.

Alcyonne had won his first two matches earlier in the morning with apparent ease, though a purple welt upon his right shoulder suggested otherwise.

During a hearty meal of pheasant and vegetables, quaffing mead by the urn, Javen and Helvius shared a good rapport. Alcyonne studied them with great interest, laughing every time Javen or Helvius laughed, even though he obviously hadn't a clue what was being said. From time to time Alcyonne tried to enter the conversation, but his efforts to make the other two understand him proved fruitless. Still, he laughed hysterically at many of the things he said.

With the meal eaten, minstrels took over the centre of the hall, relating hero's tales of yore, while bards spun yarns of bygone tournaments. All the while, jesters frolicked and tumbled throughout the room, delighting one and all.

Javen laughed at the antics of a specific jester. The little man had just recited a short poem of ill repute to the three of them, finishing his act with a back flip off their table and onto the floor.

As the jester moved on, Javen's attention was drawn to Alcyonne, bent over double and slapping his thighs, laughing so hard tears fell from his cheeks.

Javen looked at Helvius, raising his eyebrows in question.

Helvius leaned forward to get a better look at Alcyonne. Shaking his head, he sat back in his chair and shrugged.

They both sniggered tentatively, trying to restrain themselves, but couldn't. They erupted simultaneously with laughter of their own at the innocence of their newfound friend. Their laughter, in turn, set Alcyonne off even harder than before.

Their ruckus drew the attention of nearby tables. Conscious of the spectacle they were making of themselves only caused them to laugh harder.

By and by, they stifled their unbridled mirth, nursing sore ribs and drying wet cheeks.

Helvius stood, his towering height and thick torso attracting attention of those around him. Ignoring the scrutiny, something he had done his entire life, he offered a huge hand to Javen, who stood to accept the meaty handshake.

"Well, Master Javen Milford," Helvius' deep voice resonated. "I have heard many tales of your people from those of other kingdoms, and I am afraid to say, most of what I heard was not nice."

Javen's eyes widened at the man's candour. He searched for something to say, but Helvius stayed him, by holding up his free hand.

"Fear not. During my travels, I have learned not to hold much sway with another man's words. I will say, I have been in Zephyr but a short while, and though I have had little interaction with your people, if they are anything akin to yourself, those rumours couldn't be further from the truth. You strike me as a man of integrity and good manner. Thank you for allowing the likes of myself, and indeed, our laughing friend here, to share your company."

Helvius' friendly, but firm, handshake threatened to crush Javen's strong hand.

Trying not to wince, Javen was visibly relieved when Helvius let go. Humble to the core, he merely smiled and nodded his thanks.

The Serpensian stepped around Javen to regard Alcyonne with an affectionate grin. Alcyonne's wide smile parted to reveal a big set of perfectly aligned, ivory teeth.

In his haste to stand, the jovial man from Aldebaran managed to upturn his heavy chair.

Helvius laughed and extended his hand, only to be taken by surprise when Alcyonne suddenly jumped and wrapped his gangly arms tightly about him; unsuccessfully trying to lift him from the floor. Helvius looked over his shoulder at Javen, raising his eyebrows helplessly.

Javen smiled back. He and Helvius had certainly found a gem of a friend in Alcyonne.

Alcyonne released his hold on Helvius, and the larger man said, "I wish you both well this afternoon. I truly hope we need not face each other. At least not 'til the end."

"Luck to you, Helvius."

Alcyonne had no idea what had been said by either party, but he knew they were parting company. He gripped Javen in a bear hug, this time successfully lifting his victim's feet from the wooden floorboards with some effort, stumbling back under the sudden weight. He released Javen and stood back, his infectious smile replaced by a look of sincerity.

"Yaw bre," He uttered in a gravelly voice, as he looked sadly at the ground between them.

Javen and Helvius looked at each other, touched. In unison, having no idea what they were saying, they replied, "Yaw bre."

The Royal Tournament

Chapter 4 - Simply Noble

"**Hear** ye, hear ye. His Majesty, King Peter Svelte would like me to introduce to you, Sir Graham Fishon, hailing from the troubled region of Ember Breath, and his challenger, Alcyonne, hailing from Aldebaran, an oceanic realm south of Zephyr," the town crier announced before scurrying back to his seat upon a crate against the wall separating the field from the eastern stand.

The smile splitting Captain Korn's usual blank expression threatened to expose his teeth. The spectacle unfolding before him similar to that which took place earlier in the day.

A knot of squires and pages grunted and groaned, working feverishly to outfit their ever-fidgeting charge.

Javen, for his part, bore their irksome ministrations like a horse did flies. He peeked through the northern pavilion tent flaps at the backside of the knight and his horse who had just vacated the marshalling tent Javen occupied. Fishon had seemed such an ungrateful bore, going on about how his armour wasn't polished enough and berating his retainers for taking too long to outfit him.

"Come forth if thou darest, dark horseman, and know thee well, this day shall match thy colour. Surrender now and perchance I shall find in me a mercy absent my usual want. What sayest thou?" the knight's booming voice sounded mockingly from outside the northern pavilion.

Slitting the tent flaps farther apart to afford himself a better look, Javen watched as the southern pavilion tent flaps pushed outward, revealing the ebony rider. Alcyonne rode bareback atop a mottled palfrey; off-white with rusty splotches.

To Javen's astonishment, Alcyonne was clad only in the same crude leather chest protector and loose-fitting loincloth he wore at the noonday feast, a battered wooden shield his only real means of protection. He bore no other clothing or markings, save the nasty purple welt upon his right shoulder, and the well-used scorpion flail tucked into the thong cinched at his waist.

His horse bore no attire whatsoever. In fact, only Alcyonne's wide, toothy smile and intense, white and light brown eyes broke the drabness of his overall appearance.

Alcyonne rode his mount to the beginning of the tilting rail. The horse pranced uncertainly, shying from the boisterous crowd on either side of the pitch. The spectators, familiar with the dark horseman from the morning tilts, cheered louder for the foreigner than they did for the knight from Zephyr's southernmost port.

Alcyonne's eyes radiated excitement; his response to his opponent's taunting hail, a bellowing laugh. The crowd echoed his sentiments, no one realizing Alcyonne hadn't understood a single word spoken to him.

Covering his mouth, Javen stifled a laugh of his own, much to the displeasure of his retainers.

Fishon sat astride a large, black stallion. Both rider and mount were adorned in brilliant cherry-red surcoats of glistening satin that refracted the sunlight in shimmering waves, a rich green volcano, erupting violently in yellows, oranges and reds embroidered upon their surcoats. He was clearly rattled by his adversary's response, his flushed mien sporting a full, black beard. So, too, were his burly retainers, their offended faces redder than their coat-of-arms.

Javen realized Alcyonne didn't have a single retainer.

"Mock me now, black man, but let it be known, any mercy I usually afford a worthy opponent will not be accorded thee!"

Alcyonne laughed aloud.

The crowd responded in turn.

The knight looked toward the king's box, only to be affronted by King Peter's poor attempt at masking his smile.

The knight's obvious outrage only served to stir the crowd up even more.

Disgusted, the knight snatched the conical helm from his saddle horn and slammed it home upon his head, not bothering to lift the faceplate. He cantered his mount to the king's box to offer his lance;

the small vermillion ribbon from his morning victory flapping in the breeze.

Alcyonne steered his horse toward the centre of the grandstand. His huge smile elicited cheers from both sides of the field as he turned his head this way and that, pointing and winking affectionately at many different people within the crowd; not one did he know.

The knight from Ember Breath positioned his mount to obstruct his challenger, forcing Alcyonne to approach the royal box further to the right than was politically correct, causing the man-at-arms on that side to step closer to the king.

The dark warrior's eyes narrowed at the slight, but he never lost his smile. His eyes opened wide again as he looked directly into the king's, reflecting the warmth he received.

The Ember Breath man pulled off his helm long enough to nod to the king.

Both contestants offered their lances out of respect for the monarch. Alcyonne had to stretch his left arm uncomfortably to accommodate his position, his arm shaking visibly with the pull of the extended weight.

To the Ember Breath knight's chagrin, the king's gaze never strayed from Alcyonne. King Peter regarded the Aldebaranite warmly for some moments before giving him a gentle wave of his hand. The king then turned to the man on his right and began an animated conversation, obviously ignoring the knight.

With a nasty sneer directed at the black man's back, the knight snorted derisively, and cantered his horse back toward the northern pavilion.

Jarr-nash, the king's champion, looked around the king, pretending to listen, and studied the withdrawal of the rider from Aldebaran with interest.

The Ember Breath knight wheeled his mount around the northern end of the tilting rail and reined to a stop. Raising his faceplate, he bellowed, "Heed thee well, burnt man from some minor fiefdom. I will answer your mocking impertinence."

The Royal Tournament

The knight slammed his faceplate shut with a loud chink, awaiting the king's signal. The jeers heard coming from the stands did nothing to alleviate his seething.

Alcyonne cantered his mount into position. He had no idea what his opponent had said to him, but he knew by the tone, it was less than complimentary.

Alcyonne lost his smile, his heavy brow lowering over intense eyes. With a growl, he muttered between clenched teeth, "Yaw bre."

Javen's breath caught in his throat, gripping the tent flap tighter.

His retainers turned and walked away in disgust. There would be no prospect of dressing him until the present joust ran its course.

All eyes turned to watch the king's dangling white glove. After nodding to each competitor, he released it.

The crowd erupted as the horses set into motion, churning clods of earth in their wake; the horse from Ember Breath charging well before the glove hit the ground.

Alcyonne's lithe frame tensed in anticipation, his usually happy eyes narrowed, almost hidden below an uninterrupted brow, the tumultuous crowd a distant hum in his ears. His mind focused upon the oncoming rider, who still hadn't lowered his lance.

Alcyonne had jousted many times in his life. Every move came to him without thought. Approaching the impact zone, his lance tip leveled itself of its own accord. With impact imminent, his mind screamed at him. Something was wrong. His opponent's style wasn't right.

Everything happened in quick succession. From the white glove signaling the start of the joust to the impending collision, there was little time to rationalize what was happening. Instinctively, at the moment he should have been ramming his lance home, Alcyonne attempted to block his opponent's lance tip from taking his head off, but missed. He drew his left shoulder up and out, arching his back and craning his neck sideways, practically unhorsing himself in a desperate attempt to avoid the sharpened lance tip whizzing by his cheek by less than a whisper.

The crowd uttered a collective gasp, holding its breath until Alcyonne managed to regain his balance and right himself upon his horse's bare back at the rail's far end. Everyone present noted the Ember Breath knight's intent to behead his opponent.

Governed by few rules, jousting combatants followed an unwritten code of ethics. Intentionally targeting the head was frowned upon. Headshots occurred from time to time, but customarily, the knight delivering them found himself run out of the tournament if the blow was deemed anything but accidental.

Alcyonne slowed his mount, rounding the northern end of the tilting rail, readying himself for his second pass.

"Go, Alcyonne," Javen called out. "Take him out."

Alcyonne averted his gaze from the business at hand long enough to afford Javen a quick, 'watch this,' wink.

Both riders stopped their mounts before their opponent's staging area, and looked to the king.

The king stood, nodded to both riders, who in turn nodded back, indicating they were good to carry on. With a chopping motion, King Peter signaled the second pass.

Javen pulled the tent flaps together, reopening them when the churned turf ceased pelting the canvas. His eyes adjusted in time to see Alcyonne's receding posterior erect upon his mottled steed.

The charging Ember Breath knight leaned over his mount's neck, lance tip wavering at shoulder height.

Javen gritted his teeth, clenching the tent fabric so hard his knuckles turned white. His mind screamed at Alcyonne, 'get down!'

A hush fell over the crowd, many echoing Javen's thoughts.

Instead of dropping his lance to his side as he neared his competitor, the Ember Breath knight lodged the hilt into a seam in his saddle, anchoring it. Keeping the tip up, he watched for the opportunity to slip his spiked coronal above his opponent's guard so he could tear the burnt man's head off.

Bracing for impact, the Ember Breath knight's lance tip zipped harmlessly overhead.

Alcyonne's low riding coronal found its way between the plates of his opponent's thigh armour, burying itself into the knight's quadriceps, lodging deep within the man's flesh. The collision was so intense the offending lance pulled the knight's femur free of its socket, shattering his hip bone, as well as the lance, with a resounding crack.

The angry knight was shocked when his opponent's lance ripped into his groin—the pain so acute he was unable to scream. The sound of splintering wood and the whinny of his rearing horse were all that he heard as the brute force of the shattering lance turned him violently in his saddle—the broken shaft refusing to release its hold upon the gory wound it had opened within him.

He toppled from his flailing steed with a length of jagged wood protruding between the folds of plate armour covering his thigh. The last thing he remembered as he fell from his saddle was his back impacting the tilting rail, bouncing him like a rag doll to the jousting field below.

The bedlam in the crowd died off at the realization of the dire spectacle unfolding before them.

Javen winced as the knight fell spine first onto the tilting rail, the unmistakable sound of the man's spine breaking, horrific.

The Ember Breath knight thudded lifeless to the pitch.

Alcyonne watched helplessly as his lance found its mark and went to work, appalled at the ensuing ramifications of his premeditated strike. Releasing his broken lance and without regard to his own welfare, he leapt free of his running mount. Landing briefly on his feet, his momentum caused him to tumble head over heels and roll sideways several times.

His body hadn't stopped careening before he was on his feet, dirt stuck to his sweaty skin. Sprinting back to the impact site, he slipped under the tilting rail in one fluid motion and slid to the broken knight's side before anyone else had time to react.

By the time the fallen knight's retainers reached them, Alcyonne had removed the man's cherry-red surcoat, using it to staunch the incredible blood loss evidenced beneath the stricken competitor.

A burly man sporting a well-kempt goatee dropped to his knees, shouldering Alcyonne out of the way, making no attempt to acknowledge the aid the Aldebaranite had initiated.

Alcyonne considered the man without a trace of malice.

The Royal Tournament

Another man from Ember Breath ran up, yelling, "Shove off, darky, haven't you done enough damage already?"

Alcyonne looked at the ground, saddened. He couldn't understand the man's words but he surely understood their tone. Head hung low, he walked slowly down the tilting rail to gather his mottled steed, the shabby horse held by two of the Millsford stable hands working the grounds.

The crowd fell deathly quiet during the aftermath of the collision, but as Alcyonne led his horse toward the royal box, people started to chant, slowly at first, and building in crescendo as he neared the king, "Aldebaran. Aldebaran."

Standing before the king, a groom rushed over to Alcyonne, handing him the remains of his shattered lance.

Alcyonne accepted the lance with a slight nod. Lance in one hand and reins in his other, he dropped to his knees, lowering his chest to the ground, his hands stretched out before him in respect.

The two rigid knights standing guard on either side of the king's box kept a close eye on the man's strange behaviour.

All the while the crowd chanted, "Aldebaran. Aldebaran."

King Peter regarded the prostrate warrior for long moments, letting the respectful cadence from the crowd wash over the field.

The crowd ceased its cadence when the king stood to speak.

"Though I doubt you understand the words I speak, I shall speak to you so that the people gathered here may bear witness."

The king motioned with upturned palms for Alcyonne to rise.

The groom who handed Alcyonne his lance was walking away, but he noticed the man's hesitation. He walked back and reached down, gently pulling on the dark man's arm.

Alcyonne took the cue. Getting to his feet, he regarded the king with solemn reverence.

"You need not lower yourself to me, noble warrior from Aldebaran. The way you conduct yourself sets you above the morality of most contestants. The respect and courtesy you afforded your opponent, though he goaded, taunted, mocked and disrespected you, speaks volumes to your character. Arise Alcyonne. Accept your victory ribbon."

32

The Royal Tournament

Alcyonne bowed deeply, adjusting the lance in his grip so he could offer the king the hilt; his bare right hand wrapped around the sharp wreckage of the lance's shaft. The ruined tip, bloodied and dirty, bearing his earlier ribbons, lay discarded beside the fallen knight.

King Peter nodded his appreciation of the gesture and tied a small vermillion strip of cloth onto the lance's well-worn grip.

Alcyonne bowed deeply a second time and then spoke with a solemn, courtly voice that only the people near the king's box could hear, though no one understood.

The king replied, "I know not what you said." Glancing over his shoulder, he said under his breath to Jarr-nash, "You may have just told me to go get poleaxed."

It was all his bodyguard could do not to laugh.

The king's voice resumed its formal tone, "Though I am certain it does me honour. I thank you. Your actions today bring honour to your people. I say, well fought, warrior from Aldebaran."

Alcyonne waited a moment to be sure the king was done, before simply saying, "Yaw bre."

That said, he turned gracefully and marched toward the southern pavilion, leading his horse by command only. As he walked by the fallen knight it looked as though the puddle of blood beneath the man had grown larger.

The knight's attendants scowled at him, their dire looks not boding well for the knight's future.

Someone in the crowd had overheard Alcyonne's last words to the king, and started chanting. The enraptured crowd picked up the refrain.

"Yaw bre. Yaw bre."

The Royal Tournament

Chapter 5-Thwart

"**Javen!**" Captain Korn's voice brought Javen's attention back to the task at hand. Javen grunted, not wanting to take his eyes off the receding form of his friend. After Alcyonne disappeared from view, Javen turned to see the frustrated looks of his retainers and the oddly smiling Captain Korn.

"Sorry," Javen offered weakly, receiving raised eyebrows of skepticism in return, the tight-lipped faces not amused.

Captain Korn enjoyed the whole spectacle of the tournament, having worked at them, competed in them, and simply been around them for as long as he could remember. He knew well the surging emotions surrounding the event. The frustration of overworked, underappreciated squires. The ecstasy of victory and the depths of anguish in defeat. He fondly recalled the fellowship and the bitter rivalry. The last contest had encompassed all of these qualities. That's what made the Royal Tournament special.

Hearing the scurrying of field attendants outside the tent and the crier's jingling approach, the captain jumped into action, marshalling Javen's retainers to complete their tasks.

Stirred into a frenzy from the joust before, the cheering of the hometown fans followed Javen onto the field.

Captain Korn bowed deeply toward the king's box before turning smartly, following Javen's retainers back to the northern pavilion, leaving his charge to fend for himself.

Touted as one of the heavy favourites in the Royal Tournament's all-round category, Javen's opponent was deemed by many as being the only one capable of usurping Prince Malcolm's title of Master of Lance on the tilting ground, and vying for the competition's overall title, Emperor of the Field.

Korn was tight lipped. This may well be Javen's last joust. From the corner of his eye he espied Javen's splendid golden surcoat, the sword breaking upon a chaff of wheat along with his first-born label, all brilliantly embroidered with silver thread. With a wry grin, he thought the colour and design of the Milford coat-of-arms second only in magnificence to that emblazoned upon the royal standard.

Javen took control of Sunseeker's reins and turned the shiny black stallion toward the king's box, awaiting the king's nod. His right gauntlet firmly held his lance upright, the vermillion ribbon of victory fluttering beneath the coronal.

This time around he appreciated the crowd's enthusiastic support and smiled from ear to ear, but inside he concentrated for all he was worth, steeling himself to approach the king.

King Peter greeted him with a warm smile, nodding permission for the next joust to commence.

Turning his mount to face the southern pavilion, he called forth his next competitor, "Enter God's blessed field, meek challenger, if thou darest. Ride forth and know thee well ye shall face the wrath of the chaff. The eternal giver of life in a world where mere men such as thee simply come hither to wither with the passing season." Javen spoke with more vigour and confidence this time.

The crowd's exuberance fed off their local entrant's enthusiasm.

The southern pavilion tent flaps parted, pulled aside by two flamboyantly dressed retainers clad in Gritian livery, a town of mystical renown nestled in the foothills north of the Undying Wall. The knight and his mount were draped in deep forest green surcoats, emblazoned with a brilliant yellow picture of twelve high backed chairs surrounding a golden eye, depicting the Chamber of the Wise.

The Chamber, consisting of thirteen elders, oversaw the kingdom's welfare by dedicating themselves to the lore of realm. The council did not enact laws regarding the kingdom's affairs, but they had the king's ear when heavy decisions were to be made.

The Royal Tournament

The green knight's stallion, larger and more magnificent than Javen's own, trotted proudly across the field, its rider not once glancing in Javen's direction. At the king's box the knight dismounted, lance in hand, alighting upon the jousting pitch without a sound; amazing considering the amount of burnished bronze plate peeking out beneath his green surcoat. Many young ladies around the king's box swooned at his approach.

Dropping to one knee and bowing his head, he offered his lance to King Peter in mock surrender.

"Arise, noble Thwart." The king gave him a warm smile. "Your service to your kingdom precedes you. I would be amiss to deny you your sport."

Avarick Thwart, the Gritian knight, recently celebrated his seventeenth birthday and already he had proven himself a man to be reckoned with. The young knight recently led an expedition to repel a formidable raiding force pillaging the coastal towns along Zephyr's remote west shore. The men under his command suffered minimal losses while meting out the king's justice; killing over six hundred grizzled, seafaring warriors and capturing a hundred and fifty more, all the while sending the raiding ships to a briny grave.

Avarick was touted by many as the heir apparent to Jarr-nash Sylvan Jordic, the present-day king's champion and personal bodyguard. Those close to the king, however, considered him a cocky, rash young man who would stop at nothing to achieve his own ends. These sentiments were rarely spoken aloud, and certainly never when Avarick was about.

Avarick rose to his feet, offered his king a deep bow, and deftly remounted in a flourish of forest green.

Adjusting himself in his finely tooled saddle, he nodded to the king again, cantering his mount back to the tilting rail, close to Javen. Finally, he acknowledged Javen's presence, albeit to say low enough that only Javen could hear, "Enjoy the attention while you can. When I'm done with you, the only attention you will get will be from the healers."

The Royal Tournament

Avarick spurred his mount toward the marshalling area in front of his ready tent. With precise movements, he walked his horse to his starting position and waited, his stare, intimidating.

In the king's box, seated on the king's immediate left, Prince Malcolm elbowed his younger brother, Prince Nicholas, in the ribs. "Headstrong, that one."

Prince Nicholas, at age sixteen, looked much like his older brother, though his hair was a shade darker. He took his gaze from Avarick Thwart, noting Prince Malcolm's look of disapproval. Raising his eyebrows, he said anyway, "Nah, 'tis confidence, clearly. The kid's that good."

"Humph," was all Prince Malcolm said to that. Behind him sat the squire with the bewitching eyes; an oddity for one of his station to occupy a seat in the Royal Box.

Javen stared after his competitor, not knowing what to do. The Gritian knight was supposed to offer a rebuttal, but one was obviously not forthcoming. Feeling uncomfortable, he tried not to look to the king for direction, but ended up doing it anyway.

The king shrugged.

Javen sighed and turned Sunseeker toward the northern pavilion. Reaching the preordained starting location, he spun his black warhorse to face his challenger. Perhaps now the Gritian knight would respond.

Avarick grabbed his polished, conical helm from where it rested upon the pommel of his sword, placed it upon his head, and waited.

Javen swallowed, and declared weakly, "Ware thee well, good challenger, for ye are to know the heart of the chaff, for neither drought nor flood can deny it."

Captain Korn's voice reached him from behind, "Deep breath, Milford. He's trying to get into your head. Hit him low, and hit him hard. You're stronger than he is."

Javen tried to locate his mentor, but the buzz of the crowd dropped to an expectant hiss; it was time to get on with it. Turning his attention to the king's box, he was just in time to see the white glove hit the ground. At the opposite end of the tilting rail, his opponent had already commenced his charge, Thwart's mighty horse throwing clods of dirt into the air, muscles rippling, head bobbing, its forest green surcoat flapping beneath its rider's wildly spurring legs.

Javen set his heels to Sunseeker and the horse lunged forward, jamming Javen into the cantle. Regaining control, Javen settled into his saddle and concentrated upon the task at hand, though the transition didn't allow much time for thought. He lowered his lance in preparation for the inevitable collision.

Low and hard. Captain Korn's voice echoed in his head.

Avarick Thwart watched his opponent's lance tip dip and rise again. He smiled mentally. The dip was a ploy. His nimble reactions with his shield to counter the last second elevation of his opponent's tip would prove to be the hometown entrant's undoing. He raised his shield accordingly, making a subtle change to his lance's bearing, only to have his world explode into excruciating, bone crushing pain.

Javen perceived the slight adjustment of the Gritian knight's shield just before they collided. Deftly adjusting the angle of his lance tip, he drove it home, catching the surprised knight on the left pelvis. The violent impact toppled the stricken man over the rear of his mount to land heavily upon his back; the impact of his helmet with the field reverberating across the grounds.

The crowd went wild.

Maintaining a strong grip on his lance, Javen tried hard to contain his beaming smile as he turned to watch Avarick roll twice upon the field. Further up the field, Captain Korn jumped up and down, his arms flailing over his head in excitement.

After accepting his victory ribbon, Javen wheeled Sunseeker around and trotted him toward the rear of the northern pavilion, eager to be out of the public eye. Passing the green knight on the way, he paused to make sure the man was okay.

Avarick refused to acknowledge him at first. He had truly believed he would carry the jousting portion of the tournament. He was thoroughly disgusted he hadn't made it through the first day. Slapping dust from his surcoat, he shrugged off the men who came to his aid.

"Lucky blow, farm boy. We'll meet again."

Javen nodded, continuing on.

The Royal Tournament

Captain Korn took charge of Sunseeker, allowing Javen to dismount. A huge grin threatened to split the captain's face asunder.

Javen led both horse and captain around the side of the large staging tent and entered a smaller tent around the back where his retainers waited to help him out of his armour.

As he parted the tent flaps, the only warning he received before being attacked, was a maniacal shout.

The Royal Tournament

Chapter 6-Heartfelt

"Yaw bre!"

Javen stumbled backward, almost falling through the tent flaps.

Alcyonne launched himself, arms spread wide, and wrapped himself around Javen as if the two were long lost lovers.

Embarrassed, Javen returned the embrace, and with some difficulty pulled himself free.

"Heh, heh. Ya, um? Yaw bre to you, too," Javen managed, feeling more than a little uncomfortable in front of the curious stares he received from his retainers. "I think."

Alcyonne enveloped Javen's right hand with both of his, shaking it vigorously and spouting unintelligible words in his native tongue.

Javen smiled at the euphoric man as he attempted to rescue his captive hand before his arm was shaken out of its socket.

Captain Korn intervened, leading Alcyonne away from Javen to allow the retainers a chance to tend to their charge.

Enduring his entourage's ministrations, Javen watched the enigmatic Alcyonne as Captain Korn entertained the excited man in the small pavilion's back corner, patiently listening as the foreigner emphatically gesticulated at what the captain could only surmise was the retelling of Javen's last joust.

Javen's retainers flinched when Alcyonne slapped his hands together fiercely, jumped into the air and shouted, "*bam!*"

From that point on, Alcyonne shook his head in wonder, speaking gibberish, frequently pointing at Javen with a heartfelt appreciation for his new-found friend.

The Royal Tournament

"Nay, I drew Prince Malcolm," Helvius Pyxis lamented when Javen inquired how the large man's afternoon had gone. "I guess even a man my size isn't enough to best someone like him. He is smooth. Quick as a cat. Never saw his lance change its tilt. I felt it though, let me tell ya."

They were seated in the same section of the baron's hall as they were during the midday meal along with their mysterious friend from Aldebaran. The great hall buzzed with excitement. Contestants, special guests of the baron, and indeed those of the king, sank into a hearty feast of pheasant, boar, turkey, vegetables and fruit. The metallic clank of tankards meeting each other in greeting and congratulations were heard continuously throughout the hall.

Helvius hung his huge head in dismay.

Alcyonne left his seat and wrapped his arms around Helvius' shoulders. It was an odd sight, for he was shorter standing than Helvius was sitting. No one understood what he said, but the sympathy in his voice was unmistakable. Severing the embrace, he patted Helvius' massive left shoulder and returned to his seat, vigorously setting into his dinner.

Helvius raised his massive head, watching the Aldebaranite for a moment. Offering Javen a meek smile, he set in himself.

On the way back to the homestead that night, Javen seemed unusually quiet. Jebadiah tried many times to draw his son out of the shell he had retreated into, asking him questions about the tournament and commenting in general upon other tilts he observed from the vantage point of the stands. To all his remarks he received only distracted grunts. He frowned. Javen's silence was out of character.

The Royal Tournament

It wasn't until they tended the horses and were closing the barn doors that Javen spoke, his question catching his father off guard.

"Papa, why do people hate black men?"

Jebadiah nearly stumbled. "What?"

"Why do people despise them so?" Javen's stare so intense his father felt pinned to the closed barn doors behind them.

"Why, I-I don't rightly know, son. I suppose—"

"You saw the black man, Alcyonne, defeat that boor from Ember Breath?" Javen interrupted.

"Uh, well yes. It was quite a battle."

"Quite a battle. Quite a battle?" Javen was incredulous. "That knight was a cretin. Did you see how he treated Alcyonne? He wouldn't even acknowledge him as a competitor, let alone a human being. Standing before the king, the knight treated Alcyonne like shit stuck to the bottom of his boot!"

"Who are we to say what the knight was thinking?"

"And when Alcyonne ripped him from his saddle, who was the first person to his aid?"

Jebadiah had witnessed the joust, but Javen answered for him, "Alcyonne, that's who. After being treated like vermin, Alcyonne was the first one to provide assistance. He probably saved the ungrateful man's life."

He turned and walked toward their farmhouse.

Jebadiah stood where he was for a moment, staring after him. He couldn't recall a time Javen had been so riled up. He had also felt empathy toward the black man during the joust.

He hurried after his son. Catching him up, he placed a large hand on Javen's shoulder, applying enough pressure to cause Javen to stop and face him, just before they mounted the step leading up to the homestead's back porch.

A full moon crested the peak of the barn, illuminating the yard sufficiently for the two men to see each other. Rusty, their sheepdog, came bolting out of the darkness from behind the barn, tail wagging, tongue hanging out, barking and circling them, eager to go inside.

"Son, I saw what you saw," he paused, and then added, "why the sudden concern for someone you don't even know?"

The Royal Tournament

Javen studied his father for a time. Since his mother's passing years before, his father had been his mentor, his idol, his disciplinarian, his teacher—his friend. The community of Millsford all claimed the nut hadn't fallen far from the Jebadiah tree.

"Ever since I can remember, I have been told, not by you mind, but by others, that black men are savages. Black men are unclean, unlearned, uncouth, immoral creatures that would as soon rip your throat out as look at you. Why would my friends tell me something that wasn't true? And yet, because of what others said, although I'd never actually met one, I always thought the same."

"But?"

"Those rumors can't be farther from the truth, papa. Alcyonne is the kindest, gentlest soul I've ever met. All he does is smile and laugh. Even when the knight insulted him, Alcyonne simply smiled and went on to repay the discourtesy with kindness."

"Aye, that he did, my boy. That he did." With an arm around his shoulder, Jebadiah steered his son onto the porch.

Rusty started barking anew, his claws clicking upon the veranda's sagging deck boards.

"How can people say such things? If more people were half the man Alcyonne is, our world would be a much better place."

Jebadiah opened the back door with his free hand, patting his son on the shoulder as Javen entered the darkened interior ahead of him. "Aye son, right you are."

"Papa?" Javen's voice sounded from near the unlit fireplace across the room. A spark flared into being as Javen located the flint stone and lit the lantern beside the hearth. "It sure is getting cool outside."

"'Tis that time of year." Jebadiah bent down beside him to attend to the barren fire mantle.

"I don't think Alcyonne has a place to stay tonight."

Jebadiah grunted.

"Nor do I think he has any more clothes on his back than what he wore at the tournament."

Jebadiah, hunched over, smiled inwardly and nodded to the cold logs. Without looking over, he replied, "Be careful with the horses. We can't afford to have one turn a leg."

The Royal Tournament

Javen raced by his father, slowing long enough to hand him the flickering lantern, and bolted outside toward the barn. The cabin door banged noisily behind him, punctuated by Rusty's clamorous barking as the dog followed Javen into the night.

Though the moonlight amply illuminated the country road, Javen wasn't prepared for the vista sprawled out below him when Sunseeker crested the last hill heading into Millsford. The town was ablaze. Hundreds upon hundreds of campfires, in and around its low walls, served to keep the night at bay. Framing the man-made brilliance, the noisy Canorous and mighty Madrigail rivers sparkled with grandeur beneath the harvest moon; the froth from the confluence twinkled like magical dust in the moonlight.

He paused upon the hilltop to take in the spectacle. The faint din of raucous music reached him even at this distance, the smell of burning wood perceptible on the breeze. Never had his hometown hosted so many people, from so many kingdoms. The array of different languages and diverse cultures had enthralled him during the two meals at the baron's manor earlier in the day, but the gaiety unfolding before him now was surely going to take him outside of his comfort zone.

Sunseeker snorted its impatience, interrupting his reverie. With a contented smile, Javen heeled him to a canter as they descended into the magical mystery besieging the Madrigail valley.

Approaching the southern gates, they were stopped by the baron's men. Javen accepted their offer to tether Sunseeker to the guardhouse—the traffic inside the walls looked chaotic at best. He knew the youngest guard and they let him pass without further ado, offering him congratulatory hand slaps as he passed. Tomorrow, the archery competition and melee fighting events were set to commence and they wished him luck. With a grateful nod, he entered Millsford on foot.

The Royal Tournament

Once inside, the noise and scents overwhelmed his senses. Smoke from the many campfires hung visibly in the air, causing his eyes to water. Aromas of cooking meats and vegetables, slathered with a plethora of sauces, and topped with alien spices, wafted at him from every direction. People from different races, most he couldn't name, watched him as he passed, smiling and speaking in the grunts, moans, and clicks of their native tongues.

Games of chance were being held around many fires, surrounded by crowds of raucous men and women, betting and cheering the roll of dice, bones, teeth, and the gods only knew what.

Stumbling around, enraptured by the nightlife, Javen bumped into other people who weren't paying attention to where they were headed. For the most part, these casual meetings went without incident, but every so often the person he bumped into would raise his voice and give him more than a friendly nudge.

Javen, for his part, was too engrossed in the turmoil going on around him to concern himself about the harmless ire of those who strutted with a perpetual chip upon their shoulders. He presented a strong, intimidating presence himself.

It didn't take him long to realize that finding Alcyonne within this chaotic horde wouldn't be easy. He couldn't recall ever seeing a black man in Millsford, but tonight his attention was drawn to every black man, woman and child he encountered. None of them were Alcyonne.

He found himself the recipient of a violent two-handed shove. Managing to keep his feet, he stumbled backward into an unsuspecting man behind him. The man behind him cursed at his apparent clumsiness before continuing on his way, grumbling about the rudeness of young people.

Javen looked at the grizzled mien of the man who had tossed him backward, and gaped.

The man stood less than four feet tall, but his shoulders were just as wide. He boasted a stomach that hadn't missed a meal in many a year, but the sinews cording his crossed forearms bespoke incredible strength. A grey streaked beard touching the top of the man's green tunic above his thick chest provided his scowling face little relief beneath a thick mustache and profound eyebrows. The notched head of a massive battle-axe peeked above the man's left shoulder.

"Why don't ye look where you're going, imp? Next time ye may find yerself with a black eye."

Javen swallowed, apologized profusely, and hurried on. To his credit, the man grunted, accepting the apology, but Javen could feel the man's icy stare on his back as he lost himself in the bustling crowd.

About to give up the search and return to the southern gatehouse, he noticed Captain Korn doling out instructions to a knot of guardsmen while quaffing a large tankard of mead.

Javen politely stood a few yards away from the gathering and waited.

Korn dismissed the guards to their duties and spun to face Javen.

"Milford. What brings you to town this late at night? Shouldn't you be resting up for tomorrow's events? The archery qualifier is first thing in the morning."

"Uh, hey, captain. Um, yes, but I-I was just, um, looking for someone."

A slight smile upturned the captain's lips. "Blonde or brunette?"

"Huh?" Javen stared at the captain. Was the man daft or drunk?

Korn winked at him and he felt his cheeks redden.

"Oh no, captain. Nothing like that," Javen laughed uneasily. "I-I was, I mean, I am looking for a man…" he trailed off. That didn't sound right either.

Korn raised an eyebrow, letting him sweat a bit.

"Relax Milford. I'm just having sport with you. Who are you looking for?"

Relieved, Javen said, "Do you remember that black man in our tent today?"

Korn chuckled, "How can I forget? He's probably still talking."

"Um, ya, him. His name is Alcyonne."

"Alcyonne, huh?" Korn mused, placing a cupped hand on his chin, trying to recall whether or not he had seen the man recently. Suddenly, the hand cupping his chin snapped out and pointed at Javen's face. "Now that I think about it, I believe I did see him. He was leading that mottled horse toward the old Greene barn. The Greene's are billeting contestants and animals during the tournament. You know where the old Greene barn is, don't you?"

Javen's eyes lit up. "Yes sir. Just past the abandoned gristmill."

Javen bounded away toward the northern district of Millsford where the walls separated the city from the Canorous. He slowed to wave. "Thanks."

Korn smiled, shaking his head in bemusement. "Bah, 'tis nothing," he called back as Javen's form melted into the ambience of the night.

After a brisk walk, Javen found himself passing the deserted gristmill in Millsford's storehouse district. A part of the old stone building breached the town wall, where in bygone days it harnessed the Canorous River's frolicking current. The river flowed strongly along the outer walls, its waters tumbling from the heights of the steep eastern hills.

The grounds around the abandoned gristmill were nowhere near as crowded as the centre of town. In fact, Javen mused, the place appeared forsaken. Deep shadows clung to the sparse scrub covering the ground. The noises and smells of the rest of the town, though still perceptible, were less noticeable in this part of the city. Other than the audible flow of the Canorous, the only sounds to be heard in the relative darkness were the muffled laughter, grunts and groans from goings on within the deserted buildings around him. Of those activities Javen did not care to know.

He approached the old Greene barn pondering the irony of the large, derelict, red structure. He perceived, rather than saw, a group of people shuffling about just inside the open main doors of the building. Not wanting to interrupt the heated conversation taking place, he stopped at the side of the open door furthest from the city wall.

The Royal Tournament

Several paces beyond, in the shadows against the town wall, another group of men huddled over something large on the ground beneath a lone tree.

He leaned his head into the barn, unnoticed by the occupants standing inside, their backs to him. Several men of varying sizes milled around, watching something, or someone, on the ground before them, pointing and laughing. They were all clad in identical cherry-red livery, nodding at each other and flinging accusations of thievery and trickery at whoever was on the dirt floor of the old Greene barn.

One of the men gripped what looked like a fistful of fine chains that rustled and clicked when he shook them. Javen had seen it before, but without the thick redness that dripped off the metal links into the dirt. It was a scorpion flail, and these people were feeding it blood.

Suddenly the throng fell back a couple steps. The person on the ground jumped to his feet and tried to push past them, his retort unintelligible. The sweaty sheen of dark skin and dark, curly, short-cropped hair glinted in the flickering torchlight emanating from a few sconces along the interior walls. Javen recognized the distressed voice.

The dark man was thrown back to the ground before he could break free. One of the larger men jumped on top of him, pummeling his victim with a closed fist.

"Alcyonne!"

The commotion ceased, all eyes on Javen.

A burly man sporting a well-kempt goatee straddled Alcyonne. He paused his assault, his fist cocked in midair. He looked over his shoulder between the assembled men, catching Javen's eye. "None of yer business, boy. Best ye forget ye ever saw us, if ye gets me meaning."

Javen, larger than most men gathered there, was sure he was no match for the man pinning Alcyonne to the ground. Nevertheless, he stepped farther into the barn.

The Royal Tournament

Alcyonne's bruised and swollen eyes widened into what could only be taken as terror. He shook his head quickly back and forth, as if to warn Javen not to get involved. Blood dripped from his mouth.

The largest man in the group stepped up to Javen, driving a sausage-sized finger into his chest, halting his advance. The man's bald head tilted slightly, his eyebrows lifting above a malevolent sneer. He reeked of ale and sweat. "Ye'd best listen, boy, less'n you want what darky's gettin'."

Alcyonne bucked, trying to throw the man pinning him.

With a grunt and the sound of skin on skin, bone on bone, the big man's fist attempted to separate Alcyonne's head from his shoulders. "Stay down, you dirty whoreson."

Javen flinched, but before he could do anything, two men took hold of his arms, violently throwing him to the ground.

Javen braced his arms on the dirt floor in an effort to regain his feet, but the smaller of the two men who had thrown him down, kicked his left arm out, causing him to fall onto his side.

Javen instinctively flipped onto his back, crab-walking away from the man to create space, but the larger man matched his progress and dug a boot into his shoulder.

"I warned ye, boy. 'Tis nothin' doin' with ye. Best ya bugger off 'n forget it. I aint tellin' ye agin."

Javen refrained from getting up. Propped on his elbows, he asked, "What did he do to you?"

"Not yer concern, laddie. Best ya be leavin' it alone. Get it?"

"Does it take seven of you to lay a beating on one man?"

The men who had been standing by the tree took an interest in the new commotion and made their way over. From inside the barn, the man straddling Alcyonne said, "Not that it's any concern of yours, but this darky here tried to stole our stuff whilst we made merry in town. Now 'e's getting justice."

"No, you must be mistaken. Alcyonne wouldn't steal anything." Javen searched for a sympathetic face. "You have the wrong man."

Another man, the oldest and most sincere looking of the bunch, nodded sympathetically. "Aye lad. 'Tis truly shameful. 'e tried to make off with our jousting tackle, 'e did."

Javen perceived Alcyonne trying to shake his head in denial, but the beaten man lacked the strength to muster more than a tremble.

"No way. He has no need of your equipment. He doesn't use any."

"Humph. I begs t' differ. Seems 'e gone an' broked all his lances, an' needs new ones if'n 'e's to continue."

"No. He wouldn't—"

"How ye know what darky's think? Ye his caretaker? I been told he 'as not a one." The man on Alcyonne spat. "Ask these good folk here. They caught him trying to slink into the night with our lord's lances, they did. 'Tis probably matched with 'im in the morn an' afeared of 'im."

Javen didn't want to believe the man, but the onlookers nodded their agreement. Javen was crestfallen.

Gaining his feet without opposition, Javen shook his head in disbelief. He looked at Alcyonne.

A tear escaped one of the dark man's quickly swelling eyes.

Javen looked back at the men in the courtyard around the old Greene barn. To a man they pursed their lips, as if they, too, were sorry Javen had to find out about his friend this way. Some of the men looked away.

A voice in the crowd said acidly, "What's a matter, boy? Ya inta layin' wit' darkies now, are ye?"

Javen couldn't see who spoke, but the comment was met by laughter.

Javen took a last look at Alcyonne's battered visage. Sometimes justice could be severe.

He turned from the men before him and walked away, his feet scraping the hard dirt ground. With another shake of his head, he glanced back. The men he had talked with had rejoined their brethren in the barn. He couldn't see Alcyonne anymore. The man's battered form lay somewhere beneath the large man in the cherry-red surcoat.

Beneath the tree by the wall, he thought the lump looked like Alcyonne's horse upon the ground. It was too dark to tell if it was alive or not.

Javen trudged back toward the tented city, the smells and noises rising ahead of him. Laughter was everywhere. The darkness receded behind the flickering light of hundreds of cook fires. Men and women danced all about in various states of dress. People he had never seen before put their arms around his slumped shoulders and attempted to direct him toward their individual camps, offering him tankards of sloshing mead. Javen shrugged off the advances with a forced smile and a dejected, "No thank you."

He stumbled along, trying to rid his mind of Alcyonne. What a fool he was to care about the wellbeing of a man he didn't know, a man who had only been in Zephyr but for a few days. He sighed. Perhaps the stories of black men were true after all. He didn't want to believe it, but he couldn't say he hadn't been warned.

Still, something nagged at him. His pa hadn't seemed to agree with those racist sentiments, but thinking on it in hindsight, his father would go along with Javen's beliefs because that's what fathers did.

He wondered what kind of person could be so noble one moment, and so rotten the next? Alcyonne had been so jovial at the baron's manner. Twice. His demeanour full of warmth and happiness. And the events on the jousting pitch? Not that he had partaken in many tournaments during his short life, but never had he witnessed anyone do what Alcyonne had tried to do for his beaten adversary. And then to be caught stealing his next competitor's lances? Shameful. The trickster had pulled the wool over so many eyes.

"Milford. Javen! Javen Milford!"

A fist shot out of the crowd, grabbing Javen by the shoulder.

"Javen. Wake up."

Captain Korn's inebriated mien startled him out of the dark place he had fallen into.

"Uh, oh, captain. Sorry, I, uh, wasn't watching where I was going." He tried to pull away and keep walking. He wanted nothing more at that moment than to retrieve Sunseeker from the gatehouse and go home.

Korn's grip was iron.

"Whoa, whoa, whoa, young man. Why the long face. You look like you lost your dog."

Javen gave him a tight-lipped grimace.

"Ah, no luck with the women, eh?" He gave Javen a playful push.

"Uh, yes sir. That's it." Javen shrugged free and attempted to walk around the captain.

"Not so fast, Milford. Something's bothering my best jouster, and I mean to find out what. Can't have you moping along the tilting rail, you'll more 'n likely get your head knocked off. Kinda like you almost did with that knight this morning, eh? How would I explain that to dear old Jebadiah?" He smiled, trying to get Javen to do likewise. "Why he'd more 'n like take my head off, that's what he'd do, and no mistake."

The captain wrapped an arm around Javen's broad back and with difficulty pulled the boy close so he could whisper in his ear, "I'll let you in on a little secret. I've grown quite fond of my head."

If Javen even heard the jest, he didn't give it another thought. "It's nothing really, sir. It's just…"

"Just what?"

"It's Alcyonne, sir."

"Alcyonne?" The tipsy captain thought. "Ah, yes, Alcyonne. What? You couldn't find him? Couldn't find the barn? What?"

"Oh no, I found him alright. He was getting his teeth knocked out."

Korn's smile dropped. He tried to focus a little more seriously. "Does he need help?"

"I'd say," Javen sighed.

Korn looked poised to take up Alcyonne's plight, but Javen's next words stilled him.

"Apparently they caught him stealing his competitor's gear."

Korn frowned. "His competitor? What competitor?"

"Oh, I dunno. The stuff belonged to whomever he's supposed to be jousting on the morrow." Javen sighed. "He broke all the lances he brought with him, so..." He shrugged. "I guess you never truly know someone, eh?"

The captain regarded Javen with concern, but his attempt at remaining serious with the amount of spirits he had in his system was lost to him. He slapped Javen on the back. "Tough break, kid. 'Tis too bad, really. Strangely enough, I was developing a soft spot for the lad," Korn slurred as he turned to walk away. As an afterthought he added, "Not sure how he knew who his opponent would be, though. The king won't be drawing the lists until the midday feast following the melee round."

With that said, the captain disappeared into the festivity of the night.

Javen watched his retreat. When he could no longer differentiate the captain from the multitude of people between them, he resumed his course toward the southern gatehouse. Doing his best to avoid the amiable drunkards staggering and swaying everywhere, he pondered the captain's last words. Why would the men in the cherry-red surcoats…?

Cherry-red surcoats! The men at the old Greene barn were all clad in the same colour livery worn by that rude knight Alcyonne had faced earlier in the day. The same colours worn by the knight who broke his back upon the tilting rail; most likely injured beyond recovery.

Of course. Ember Breath colours. Those men were the same vile retainers who attended the contemptible knight on the field. The very same men who had scorned Alcyonne's attempt at aid following the collision. The man with the well-kempt goatee!

According to Captain Korn, Alcyonne would have no way of knowing who he faced the next day. Even if he did, it certainly wouldn't be the knight from Ember Breath. That knight was not only beaten, he was probably dead.

Javen's eyes grew wide. They weren't exacting justice upon a man who stole from them. They were exacting retribution upon a kind, caring man who, in all probability, even though they treated him like horseshit, had gone in search of the injured knight to see if he was okay.

Javen stopped dead in his tracks. His blood ran cold. He had left his friend to die.

Frantically looking around, he realized with a sinking feeling, there was no way he was going to be able to relocate Captain Korn in time to help. He scanned the crowd anyway, as he began to half walk, half jog back toward the storehouse district, hoping to see someone he knew. Never had he seen so many foreign faces.

The Royal Tournament

He was at a loss as to what he should do. Alcyonne's need was dire. Without another thought he started running through the jubilant masses, pushing people out of his way, absently apologizing as he did so. His shoving wasn't given a second thought by most. A few drunken knights attempted to give chase after being knocked aside, but Javen lost them in the crowd.

Jostling his way through the crowd, he tried to put the tarpaulin city festivities behind him. Preoccupied with his need to get to Alcyonne, he no longer heard the laughter and singing around him, or the loud talking of people about the various campfires. Or the voice of a friend who called out to him as he bolted past.

Within minutes that felt like hours, he left behind the tumult of the main encampment. The streets became quieter, colder, darker. The noise and exotic scents were replaced by his laboured breathing and the damp smell of dew settling upon the ground.

The long shadows on the road shortened as he passed the abandoned gristmill.

The small group of men who gathered to watch had grown in number; everyone jostling for space inside the old Greene barn, their attention riveted upon the fight inside.

Javen swallowed heavily. He would receive no help there. Most of them were clad in cherry-red apparel.

He approached the side of the barn, wondering how in the world he was going to win Alcyonne free, but the sound of skin smacking skin, and the feeble groan of despair that followed, removed any thought of subtlety.

Javen emitted an angry growl, adrenaline sloughing aside his common sense. He threw himself into the backs of the onlookers.

The startled group parted, caught unaware. They grabbed at him, but weren't quick enough.

The large man straddling Alcyonne turned his head in time to see Javen's headlong charge.

Javen threw his entire body weight into the man's shoulder, wrapping him in outstretched arms and carrying the man with the well-kempt goatee from Alcyonne's limp form. They rolled in a heap upon the dirt floor, a cloud of dust rising in their wake.

The Royal Tournament

The largest spectator took a spot atop Alcyonne ensuring the Aldebaranite didn't escape, but Alcyonne was too far gone to resist.

The older man who had berated Javen earlier, stepped between the crowd and the two men fighting, keeping the others from intervening. A wicked sneer parted his lips as he pointed to the man with the well-trimmed goatee grappling with Javen. "No one interferes. He lives for this."

It soon became apparent Javen's farmer's strength and surprise attack wouldn't be enough to contain the brute beneath him. Javen wasn't a brawler. The man squirming beneath him was.

The man with the goatee worked his way from beneath and twisted on top of Javen. He started delivering bone crunching punches to Javen's ribs, and then to his face.

Javen tried to block the brunt of the blows, but with the force that they were delivered, his efforts did little to mitigate their impact.

Thankfully, the man's assault ceased as he jumped to his feet and studied Javen's dirty, bloodied face. He spat. The rank spittle smacked upon the right shoulder of Javen's ripped tunic.

"Don't…ever...jump me…again," the man said between heavy breaths. "I oughtta…whoa!"

Javen kicked out his legs, catching the man around the ankles. With a quick twist, he pulled the man to the ground, and delivered a healthy beating of his own upon the back and side of the cowering man's head.

The toe of a riding boot cracked Javen beneath the chin, putting a quick end to the fight.

A white light went off inside Javen's head as the boot lifted him clear of the large man. Blackness ensued before he hit the ground.

How long Javen remained unconscious, he didn't know. It couldn't have been long. From his new vantage point, pinned against the riverside wall of the old Greene barn by both arms—each arm held by two sneering, foul smelling men in cherry-red livery—he could vaguely make out the blurred image of his assailant dusting himself off.

Javen smiled weakly. Blood leaked from the large thug's right ear, and judging by the look of his nose, both eyes of the man with the well-trimmed goatee would be fused shut before the sun rose again.

Javen's head lolled back and forth, his chin resting upon his chest, as he tried to watch the large man sneering back at him, through his own swelling eyes. Bloody spit drooled from his mouth. He could only imagine what was to come next. It wasn't going to be good, but he felt gratified he had taken the attention of the Ember Breath contingent away from Alcyonne, if only for a while. The kindly, good hearted man from Aldebaran hadn't deserved this.

The large man's glare promised death, his puffy eyes never leaving Javen's. He cocked his head to both sides, shaking out the large muscles in his shoulders. With a sardonic grin, he approached the foolish farm boy held against the barn's weathered planks. He delivered the first blow to Javen's midsection with such force that Javen's breath left him as his feet lifted off the ground. Even the men holding him cringed and looked away.

Through watery, pain laced eyes, Javen tried to focus upon the man reloading his right fist. This one would come for his face, he knew. He also knew he wasn't likely to survive it.

The man drew back, hopping upon his toes in preparation, rocking back to gather momentum before delivering the death punch.

A blood curdling battle cry filled the air as the man with the well-trimmed goatee left his feet, all his weight thrown behind his fist.

Only the splintering barn boards gave him pause as his head impacted with fatal force mere inches away from Javen's. He hadn't even had time to cry out, nor had he seen who had pulverized him from behind like a battering ram.

The scene in the barn erupted into pandemonium. Initially, all the men in cherry-red livery charged the man responsible for their cohort's death, but in the next heartbeat, they were turning, and fleeing for their lives.

The huge frame of Helvius Pyxis, long, greasy hair flying about his head, destroyed everyone within arm's reach. Men were knocked senseless by a single blow of his war hammer fists. Others were tossed through the air, impacting with the shaking walls and roof beams of the old Greene barn. The men holding Javen slowly, and ever so gently, lowered him to the ground, palms facing outward in submission. Their eyes were round with terror. Their pants wet with fear.

Soon all activity in the barn stopped. Dust hung in the air. Moans and whimpers from the few surviving Ember Breath men disturbed the eerie silence that settled upon the killing ground.

Javen's breath returned to him painfully. He was alive, although his vision dimmed. Outside the barn he discerned a few of the remaining Ember Breath contingent cowering in a small knot. He heard Captain Korn taking control of the scene, barking orders to unseen militiamen.

Directly before him, Helvius' massive form, hunched upon his knees, cradled Alcyonne's damaged head within his large, battered hands. The colossus gently wiped the blood away from the dark man's eyes, his own eyes watering at the damage that had been inflicted upon his friend.

Javen couldn't tell whether Alcyonne still lived, and if so, for how much longer. He tried to adjust himself into a more comfortable sitting position to see better, but found he couldn't. Stabbing pain lanced through his body. He wanted to cry out, but he lacked the strength. His vision dimmed further, his thinking hazier. He coughed up a gob of blood that slid slowly down his chin. Faintly, ever so faintly, he heard two beautiful words.

"Yaw bre."

Javen managed a weak smile before darkness claimed him.

The Royal Tournament

Chapter 7 - Emperor of the Field

Sunshine glistened along the freshly polished, oak tilting rail. An over-capacity crowd gathered to watch the final competition of the Royal Tournament: the championship joust. Amongst the many dignitaries occupying the royal viewing box, located in the centre of the east stand, two people stood out above all others. All eyes watched them. All mouths spoke of them. The heavily bandaged black man, and his equally bound, white companion. Of all the competitors in the tournament, the prince included, nobody elicited more gossip than the mysterious man from Aldebaran.

Javen and Alcyonne were given the honour of watching the final joust beside Jarr-nash Sylvan Jordic, the king's champion. Alcyonne sat on Jarr-nash's right with Javen beside him. The baron's men had replaced the original seats with wide, padded armchairs fetched from his personal study. Behind them sat the imposing Helvius Pyxis, two chairs wide, watching over them.

A week had passed since that fateful night at the old Greene barn. Javen had heard correctly before succumbing to the beating he received, it was Captain Korn who had rushed to the old Greene barn with as many of the baron's men as he could scrounge up along the way, the majority of them off duty. In the short time it took the captain and his men to get there, they found the battle already over.

Helvius had been sitting around one of the tarpaulin city's campfires and noticed Javen running toward the abandoned gristmill with grave concern written on his face. He'd tried to hail Javen, but the boy hadn't heard him. Helvius had been around men long enough to realize something serious was afoot, so he set out to render whatever assistance he could. While trying to follow Javen's trail, he informed an on-duty man-at arms about his concern regarding the baron's prized entrant.

The Royal Tournament

It had taken Helvius time to stumble across the old Greene barn, finding Alcyonne's bloodied body lying helpless upon the cold dirt floor. He arrived in time to witness the big brute deliver a rib-crushing blow to his other newly found friend restrained by four men against the red barn's far wall. Erupting in a blind rage, he nearly brought the roof of the old Greene barn down.

By the time Captain Korn and his men arrived, the surviving Ember Breath men were begging to be taken into custody.

Clad in green and red patchwork livery, the town crier announced the tournament's final joust, "Hear ye, hear ye. It is His Majesty's delight to introduce to you, Prince Malcolm, Master of Lance and reigning Emperor of the Field."

The crowd rose to their feet, their cheers drowning out the crier's announcement, "And his challenger, hailing from Storms End, Sir Nashon Oakes."

Trumpets sounded. All eyes fell on the northern pavilion, everyone eager to espy the heir to the Ivory Throne. All except the king's.

King Peter watched the bruised and battered countenances of Alcyonne and Javen. The two young men, in obvious discomfort, were somehow ignoring their pain and eagerly awaiting the arrival of the reigning Emperor of the Field, as excited as the rest of the crowd. The evening before, Prince Malcolm had drawn his younger brother in the lists and had beaten Prince Graham without much trouble.

The trumpet's staccato blare ceased as the prince trotted Firerider from the northern pavilion. After his squire had double-checked his saddle's cinches, Malcolm directed his ebony charger to the end of the tilting rail. Without preamble, he bowed low over his saddle horn; his blonde locks falling around his shoulders. Sitting up, he gave his hair a slight flick to rid it from his eyes and gazed at the southern pavilion, his right hand holding his lance at ease, perpendicular to the field.

The Royal Tournament

"Enter God's blessed field, meek challenger, if thou darest?" the prince called. "Ride forth and know thee well, today ye shall be bested by the Emperor of the Field."

On cue, the large tent flaps of the southern pavilion opened outward, pulled by two handlers in black livery; their crests, a golden sun rising above a grey storm cloud, depicted upon five golden rays of sunshine emanating from below the thundercloud, emblazoned upon their backs.

The challenger walked his ivory destrier onto the pitch. The knight sat high upon his massive horse dressed in gleaming black satin highlighted with golden thread piping. Such was his mantle, he appeared more regal than his royal adversary.

The knight spurred his mount to a trot, bringing it to a halt alongside Prince Malcolm. As custom dictated, the knight from Storms End immediately offered the Emperor of the Field his lance, hilt first, bowing low over the pommel of his finely tooled saddle.

"I submit to thee without contest should the Emperor deign it so."

The Emperor of the Field placed his left hand upon the lance handle. "Brave challenger, I would not dishonour your coat of arms without contest. Should ye decide now to withdraw from the tournament, I shan't begrudge your courage. What say ye, o' noble warrior?"

The black-clad knight pulled his lance back onto his lap. He located his helmet hung upon a thong strapped to the saddle behind him, methodically undid the tie, and placed the golden, flat-topped helm upon his large head. He flipped open the face plate and bowed his head.

"With all due respect, my liege, ward yourself well, for on this morn your storm shall end." The Storms End knight pulled on his reins, urging his ivory mount about with a fancy sidestep, and approached the royal box.

The Emperor of the Field fitted his vermillion plumed helm upon his head, and called after his challenger, "Then I say unto you, ware thee well, ye foolish knave!" He spurred Firerider after the Storms End knight.

The Royal Tournament

The crowd cheered the two riders approaching the royal box, their lances adorned with six vermillion ribbons each. The king's awning was ablaze with every coat of arms in attendance, the pennants hanging limply in the still air on either side of his own house's banner.

King Peter gave the combatants leave to assume their respective starting places.

Before Prince Malcolm spurred Firerider away, he shook the end of his lance. The tip quivered, causing a pennant to unfurl from its end. Emblazoned upon the triangular cloth was a picture of a volcano dominating a sandy island, paired with a smaller volcano dominating a second island, all upon an azure background.

King Peter smiled, wondering where in the world his son had found such an obscure flag on short notice, especially here in Millsford. He must have commissioned a cloth merchant.

Malcolm hoisted the lance high. "Aldebaran!"

The crowd thundered to its feet, chanting, "Aldebaran. Aldebaran. Aldebaran."

Clapping, King Peter looked past Jarr-nash, touched by the smiles on Alcyonne and Javen's battered faces—tears of heartfelt appreciation welling in their eyes.

Alcyonne enjoyed hearing the crowd chant his country's name. Prince Malcolm's tribute touched him profoundly, while Javen appreciated the honour the masses bestowed upon his friend.

The murmur in the stands died off, replaced by a palpable strain of curbed enthusiasm.

King Peter surveyed the hushed crowd with a smile. These were his people, and as usual, they made him proud to be their sovereign.

He pulled the white glove out from where it rested tucked into his belt and hoisted it high for all to see, large rings twinkling on the last two fingers of his right hand.

The atmosphere hummed with the enthusiasm of the crowd. Watching the glove drop, they practically fell forward with it.

The prince and his challenger adjusted their grips upon their leather-bound hafts, eyes focused upon the descending cloth. Each man took a large breath, their toes moving their stirrups forward, their secondary hands cinching their horses' reins.

The glove made contact with the turf.

The crowd roared, watching the jousters spur hard, their horses exploding into a headlong gallop, muscles rippling, nostrils flaring; earth churning.

Watching Firerider charge along the tilting rail, Javen marveled how the prince maintained such an erect posture in the saddle, with a challenger tearing down the pitch toward him intent on ripping his head off.

The knight from Storms End rode his horse arrow straight, his right hand clutching the haft of his lance, his left hand strapped to the elbow, holding his shield fast.

The first two passes ended in stalemates. The jousters shattered their lances upon their opponent's intercepting shields, both men struggling to remain in their saddles under the force of such blows.

The crowd held its breath in anticipation as the king signaled the third pass.

Prince Malcolm's mystique lay in how long he could hold his lance perpendicular to the tilting rail and keep his colourful shield resting upon his thigh, before finally dropping his lance to level with speed and control, raising his shield with equal precision, leaving the actions seemingly long past the last possible moment, affording his opponent little opportunity to gauge the tilt of his lance.

The Storms End knight, poised to dethrone the Emperor of the Field, felt his breath leave him.

A lightning quick up-thrust from Malcolm's rapidly falling lance tip evaded the unfortunate man's shield, catching him square in the centre of his breastplate. The spiked coronal crunched into the knight's polished steel plate, eliciting a tooth aching sound of scraping metal.

The Storms End knight spun his shoulders to the right in a desperate attempt to prevent the careening metal tip from slipping under his gorget—his lance shattering at the same moment upon the prince's shield. His agility allowed him to spin fast enough in his saddle to avoid decapitation, but the evasive manoeuver shifted his

The Royal Tournament

weight in the saddle enough that his mount took it as a signal to turn harder than its speed would allow. Both rider and mount fell, the collision with the earth felt in the stands.

With cool, practiced precision, Prince Malcolm regained control of his lance and hoisted the coronal high.

The crowd went delirious, screaming and ranting about the wondrous skill of Zephyr's beloved son.

Javen and Alcyonne were on their feet embracing each other, oblivious to the hurt.

King Peter knew well his son's prowess upon the jousting pitch. He merely sat and clapped, along with his second son, Prince Graham. They had seen it countless times before.

Jarr-nash, however, was on his feet, appreciating the spectacle of the prince's finesse, knowing firsthand what it felt like to be unhorsed by such a sublime, yet lightning quick strike.

Prince Malcolm trotted his horse around the southern end of the tilting rail, past the king's box, and reined Firerider in beside the visibly shaken knight from Storms End.

The unhorsed knight regained his feet with the help of his retainers and immediately attended his horse.

The prince took no offence to the apparent slight, appreciating the bond between a man and his horse.

Assured his horse was okay, the Storms End knight located his fallen lance, and approached the Emperor of the Field, helmet clutched between his left arm and body. Reaching the prince, he dropped to his right knee, and bowed his head. "I submit to thee, mine Emperor. I beseech thee, do unto me no further grief."

"Arise, Sir Nashon Oakes of Storms End. Ye have jousted well this tournament and have no need to bend your knee to me on the field. Take your shattered lance and know your skill shall be most welcome amongst the King's Guard should you wish to enlist."

"I am humbled, my liege," Oakes replied reverently, still on one knee, head bowed.

The prince turned his horse toward the royal box, hefting his lance high into the air.

The crowd cheered.

The Royal Tournament

Reaching the centre of the east stand he dismounted in a graceful flourish of billowing black, gold and vermillion robes, bending his knees slightly and landing with nary a sound. Two regal strides and a deep bow had him standing before the king.

Malcolm's squire rushed across the field with a new lance, complete with the six victory ribbons and the Aldebaran pennant. He exchanged the lance with the prince, bowed deeply to the king and scurried away.

King Peter received Malcolm's lance tip, and knotted the Emperor of the Field pennant to an open spot on the populated length of wood. The Emperor of the Field flag, red in colour, depicted a black silhouette of a knight sitting tall upon a horse, lance at ease, in relief upon a yellow background.

The king looked beyond his son to the knight walking up behind Malcolm.

"Well done, Sir Nashon Oakes. You have brought honour to Storms End."

The defeated knight bowed.

The king smiled and looked proudly upon his son. He raised his voice for all to hear, "Congratulations to this year's Master of Lance, Malcolm Alexander Svelte: Knight of the Realm, Captain of the King's Guard, and first Prince of Zephyr. For three years running have you bested all comers. There is only one knight whom has more banners than thee, and he of course, is my champion." The king paused to indicate Jarr-nash.

The crowd clapped heartily. Jarr-nash, shy as ever, stood after a bit of prompting from the king, and gave a quick wave to the crowd, causing the noise level to rise appreciably.

The king held up his hands, calming the crowd. "I also present to you, Prince Malcolm Alexander Svelte, this year's Emperor of the Field."

The masses chanted, "Prince Malcolm. Prince Malcolm. Prince Malcolm."

Bowing his head in appreciation, the prince then took everyone by surprise, vaulting over the barrier separating the field from the stands. This time he thudded heavily, his armour clanging against

64

the royal box as he came to a rest before Javen and Alcyonne. He gave Javen a quick handshake before turning to Alcyonne.

The grounds became silent as the prince addressed the injured man from Aldebaran, "As Emperor of the Field, I bequeath my position unto you, Alcyonne of Aldebaran. For through your noble display of joy and goodwill toward everyone you have encountered here this week, whether they liked you or mocked you, your actions reflect what the Royal Tournament is all about. As my good father, the king, will attest, never has anyone been treated so poorly at the hands of men of Zephyr. Their actions bring our house into disrepute. Our realm, my realm, is shamed."

He paused.

The stands were deathly still.

"I assure you, and all gathered here under the protection of the house of Zephyr, that we do not, nor will not, tolerate such actions as those perpetrated upon this noble warrior from Aldebaran. Rest assured, the men in question, at least those who survived," the prince gave the huge man from Serpens a wink, "are incarcerated, and shall face the full wrath of our good king. I have it on good authority said justice shall be swift, and if merited, most severe."

"Also, I have heard from a reliable source that you have need of a new horse and lance." The prince nodded to Javen, as he presented his finely polished, beribboned lance to Alcyonne.

The Aldebaranite looked at the lance with awe. Swallowing hard he looked straight into the prince's eyes. He didn't know what the prince had said to him, but he understood the intent. Tears rolled down his cheeks. Without warning, instead of grasping the proffered lance, and despite his injuries, he left his feet and embraced the startled prince, doing his best to squeeze the air from the prince's royal lungs.

When he finally released Malcolm, Alcyonne wrapped an arm over the prince's shoulder. He snatched the lance with his other hand and hefted it into the air, his huge smile displaying a mouth full of broken teeth.

The Royal Tournament

It was then that Alcyonne saw the magnificent, dark brown quarter horse being led from the northern pavilion. He looked at the prince questioningly, with tears in his eyes.

It was all Prince Malcolm could do not to cry himself, so he just nodded.

With a voice belying his frail condition, the Aldebaranite shouted, "Yaw Bre!"

The crowd exploded in thunderous unison.

Javen had never been as happy for anyone in all his life. He surveyed the jubilation of the crowd, and then looked to the king.

King Peter Malcolm Svelte was on his feet, clapping hard, and chanting louder than anyone else, "Yaw bre! Yaw bre! Yaw bre!"

The End...

... perhaps not.

The Royal Tournament

If you enjoyed this book, please look for, *Of Trolls and Evil Things*.

Releasing August 21, 2018 is the Epic Fantasy, *Soul Forge*, a novel about the adult lives of the characters from the two prequels, and how they came to be together as their world crumbled down around them.

Wizard of the North, book 2 in the *Soul Forge Saga,* releases September 18, 2018.

Into The Madness book 3 in the *Soul Forge Saga* releases December 2018

Please visit my website: www.richardhstephens.com
If you wish to keep up to date on new releases, please subscribe to my newsletter by clicking on the contact tab on my website. It will only be sent out on the day of a new release.

You can also look me up on Facebook:
https://www.facebook.com/RichardHughStephens/

The Royal Tournament

A little about me.

Born in Simcoe, Ontario, in 1965, I began writing circa 1974; a bored child looking for something to while away the long, summertime days. My penchant for reading The Hardy Boys led to an inspiration one sweltering summer afternoon when my best friend and I thought, 'We could write one of those.' And so, I did.

As my reading horizons broadened, so did my writing. Star Wars inspired me to write a 600-page novel about outer space that caught the attention of a special teacher who encouraged me to keep writing.

A trip to a local bookstore saw the proprietor introduce me to Stephen R. Donaldson and Terry Brooks. My writing life was forever changed.

At 17, I left high school to join the working world to support my first son. For the next twenty-two years I worked as a shipper at a local bakery. At the age of 36, I went back to high school to complete my education. After graduating with honours at the age of thirty-nine, I became a member of our local Police Service, and worked for 12 years in the provincial court system.

In early 2017, I resigned from the Police Service to pursue my love of writing full-time. With the help and support of my lovely wife Caroline and our five children, I have now realized my boyhood dream.